*Carson at the Fence Lines*

*By R. Michael Beahan*

# Copyrights

# Dedication

In memory of my parents, James and Helen Beahan

## Preface

**Carson at the Fence Lines** is a father's recollections as told to his brassy teenage daughter about the benevolence and complexities of his 1960s childhood days in the town of Carson City, Michigan, population 1,043. We Boomers recall the sixties like a slideshow of stark black and white photographs. The images are of student protests, burning draft cards, and Volkswagen Beetles set to a psychedelic soundtrack of Vietnam War protest music. These urban memories deceive us. The fact is most kids developing in those turbulent times lived in the boondocks.

Little sleepy towns are a myth. Instead, they buzz with effervescent characters, captivating community celebrations, and one-off episodes that endure long in local legend. It's the "live wires" that made growing up in Carson City a blessing. This is especially true for boyhood pal and sometimes mischief-maker Mark Monoly and his best friends Brenna, Darby, and "The Nocks". Their school, venerable and financially compromised St. Mary Academy, closes as they enter their high school years. The Catholic kids mix well in their new corporeal world but never escape the fundamentals of their catechism lessons.

As new public preps, they come of age surrounded by an exploding culture. Teachers, benevolent residents, and clergy are there guiding them through the incoherence of the late1960s. This retrospect explores the overt and subtle changing ways of life for these friends in the class of 1970. Mark and his teenage friends are models of complicity, but when conscience compels, they act out with "in your face" confrontations to those who censure their reading of **Henderson the Rain King**. Based on actual events, this fictionalized account recalls their pranks, joys, disappointments, lessons learned, conflicts, and tragedies in an era that tested the fundamental decency and virtues in the heartland.

## Table of Contents

## Chapter 1 *The Snowball*

"How about I drive?" Molly says with an impish grin as she plops herself down in the driver's seat of our bright red and very cool Jeep Wrangler. With her brand-new restricted teenager driver license, she needs all the supervised driving experience her mother and I can give.

It's hard to believe when she got behind the wheel of the Jeep for the first time just a few weeks before, she could shift the manual 4 speed transmission as if she were a veteran million-mile Teamster. It's a puzzler to watch her shift it so very well but, for some crazy reason, she can't steer a vehicle straight on a road to save her life. I label her driving skills an "oxymoron".

When she's driving, she scares us to death by meandering over the center line or going the other direction and slipping a tire off the right shoulder of the road. Her mother and I hope that it's just a matter of her getting more driving experience that will literally "straighten her out." Her chauffeuring me through the State of Michigan to my hometown will be good driving practice for her. God knows she needs it before we turn her loose and unsupervised to drive among the unsuspecting motoring public. "Let me text your mom so she'll know we've left," I say as she pulls out of the driveway and heads up our street. "Texting", I declare, "is such a great way to inform family of our whereabouts." Then, like any dorky dad, I couldn't resist throwing in the qualifier "We didn't have texting when I was a kid."

Before she can roll her eyes in teenage exasperation and also to have a little fun with her, I double it down and bait her further. "Back in the good old days," I tell her, "none of our parents knew much what we teens were doing once we departed to some destination." To that I add yet another, "When I was a kid", followed by my explanation that when we reported any change of plans when we filed our post travel variance reports, our moms and dads became very skeptical.

Molly is up for the fun and sees the opening to put a dig on her dad. She teases that "It was tough being a kid back in the Stone age eh Dad?" Laughing, I answer, "I guess every parent says this but yes, when I was your age growing up was a way different experience."

Molly is, at age 16 bright, inquisitive, a great communicator. She dazzles in a conversation. She could put a Pulitzer Prize winning investigative reporter to shame the way she asks so many thoughtful and inquisitive questions. Other times she just wants to poke the dad bear, but never with malice. Teenage Molly loves lively discussions and mocks everyone, including and perhaps more than anyone else, her dad. Her teasing is always good-natured and her intentions are always to be funny, nothing she says would cause someone she targets to have hard feelings.

Molly decides this is a good traveling topic and asks, "So how was it for you Dad, growing up in a tiny farm town like Carson City?" She follows with the zinger, "Did you and your pals tip over cows for fun?"

This is Mocking Molly at her best and it makes me laugh. "No cow tipping," I counter, then I turn the conversation into a more serious tone. "But it was different growing up in a small town in the late 60s. I think the Vietnam War was the main influence in those years. Youth come pre-packaged as rebellious, but the War permeated into every one of our experiences, it was a daily invasion into our lives. Nothing had a greater influence on my generation than the War in Vietnam. It turned us into a hostile, irreverent, and insubordinate generation. The tumultuous culture the War in Vietnam created reached us even in the little Podunk of a town where I came of age." Molly seemed interested in this so I expanded the thought.

"The way my folks raised me differs from the way your mom and I are parenting you.", I declare. "How's that, she asks," as our Jeep buzzes by the green and silver city limits sign of rust belt Muskegon. I think a minute before answering as we set our course to the East in the bright spring morning sun.

The puffy clouds of a morning storm are behind us now and the sky has turned a deep morning blue, the wind inland slowed now to a typical Michigan breeze. After gathering my thoughts, I gave her my serious answer. "Above everything else, my parents were devout Catholics. That's quite a contrast to your Mom and I. You know we're very moderate on issues of religion. But in my childhood the Catholic Church was, next to my parents, the most influential facet of my upbringing."

I see she's interested, so I continue my thoughts and recollections. I start by telling Molly that my earliest memories as a child are of my Mom and Dad taking me to Mass at St. Mary's Church. Going to church wasn't my choice, but the iron-clad family rules.

St. Mary's is an elegant piece of the 1800s architecture. The church's beauty is rare for a small town like Carson City. Irish immigrants built the exterior of St. Mary's out of rich, solid bright red brick and even today, the church is by far the tallest and most impressive building on the local landscape. Brick buttresses secure the great height of the church. They hold up her long tall sides and the patterned green shingled steep roof. A great spire pierces the sky above and it's topped just like almost every Catholic church going all the way back to St. Peter's in Rome, with a simple white cross.

The venerable church towers over the town full of

regal mature silver maple trees and a scattering of tall white pines. These long-standing trees shade the old homes and the aging brick buildings that house a modest handful of family-owned shops on Main Street. The steeple is visible from the surrounding farmlands, crosscutting the skyline as if marking its place in the heavens. Below the belfry is a large 4-face black clock with elegant gold hands and classic Roman numerals. The clock displaying the time to the north, south, east and west. The century old bronze church bells to this day ring out to the flat plain to the east and south of town and the low rolling hills to the west and north. If this Church was a person, she would be a giant with hands on her hips, shoulders square, jaw jutting out with boundless confidence, her eyes fixed on the horizon as if to say, "I am the center of everything." For my fellow Catholic friends and I growing up in Carson City, St Mary's Church was the epicenter of our young lives.

A short city block to the East of the Church, past St. Mary's Hall, was the Catholic school we all attended. The school, St. Mary's Academy, the church founders originally built to be the Dominican Nun's Convent. But because of an adequate supply of cheap labor (the Dominicans) and an oversupply of unplanned Catholic children, the parish converted it to a K through twelve school in 1903. St. Mary's Academy was an impressive two stories tall and made from the same red bricks as was the priest's rectory and the Church. In this school we Catholic children, two and sometimes three classes crammed into a single

11

classroom, sat and learned. The pious Dominican Sisters covered all the typical school subjects. The one exception, and the most important class they taught, was Catechism.

The nuns in those days wore the traditional black and white robes with black laced boots, a white habit, a jet-black veil, and always, the long black rosary beads cinched to their waists. The iconic black and white medieval gowns made it easy for the school children to nickname them the "Penguins," a name even our parents called them with affection. Teaching nuns have reputations of being strict and cruel, but our experience was that they were gentle. They transfixed us kids with New Testament stories of Jesus's great miracles and the horror of the Passion. The nuns were devout, lived simple lives of self-denial, and taught us how we could gain our ultimate reward in heaven through the grace of the Church. No exceptions.

School started at 8am sharp every weekday during the school year. But before the first class of every school-day, Church policy required each student from all grades to attend the half hour 7:30am morning Mass, a short walk from the school. We children took in the Mass every morning, praying under the soft amber light that radiated down from the tall stain glass windows on each side of the church. They organized us in pews separated by class and gender with a nun in the first seat in each row to suppress any mischief-making. There we prayed out loud in Latin alongside those venerable old windows inscribed with the names of the oldest families in the parish, the O'Conner's, O'Brien's, Flannigan's, Donahue's. The honorable founder's names on the windows lit up in the morning sunlight as we worshiped and made our small prayers. It was as if these long dead Irish immigrants who came to Michigan, settled in this small town, then built this Church, were, from these towering windows, in a perpetual protective watch over us.

The nuns told us the names of our ancestors on those windows were like messages from heaven. They said that those founding members had earned their place in heaven and are there waiting to welcome us to eternity. The nuns taught us that, after we'd died and our souls proceeded to heaven, our empty shelled bodies would be forever lying beside them just a few blocks away at Maryknoll, our little Catholic Cemetery. The nuns taught us that our lives were just a temporary test of faith and our eternal reward was waiting for us in heaven. They taught us getting to heaven was easy. We could get there by being obedient and giving service to God through the Church. They made sure, with graphic descriptions, we understood Hell was not our destination of choice.

It wasn't long into our Catholic education that the Church gave three of us third-grade boys a special opportunity to volunteer for the Church. The nuns phoned our parents and told them that with their permission and support, their sons could become altar boys. Normally, no boy could become a server until reaching the fifth grade, but as the nuns explained, our selection came straight from Father, and he had prayed on it. Any 8-year-old singled out by the Parish Priest gave the family a special status in the Church. To have a third grader serve Mass put the boys on full display in the parish and a testimony to their good parenting. The nuns and the parish priest determined that we were mature for our age, and most of all, that our parents were doing a good job raising us up as proper Catholics.

Until this point, Father and the nuns communicated with the parents on the down-low. We boys were the last to know that the three of us would become the newest and youngest altar boys.

When Father contacted our parents, they gave their permission without hesitation. Within a few days, he started the process to start our indoctrination as the 3 youngest altar boys.

Sister Ann, a diminutive Dominican nun who taught in the High School upstairs, came to our third-grade classroom to make a "very important" announcement. She was beaming and announced to the 30 of us in the class of 1970 that there were three special boys that Father O'Brien was requesting to come over to the rectory. His purpose was to meet with them about becoming altar boys. She called Mark Monoly, Richard Gusnoki, (Richard or Dick to adults, "The Nocks" to the rest of us), and I. She called us to follow her out the front door of the creaky old school and over to the rectory to meet with Father.

Father Ralph O'Brien was a 60-year-old "Black" Irishman with a ruddy complexion and jet-black hair that swept straight back over his round head. He was stocky and athletic looking except for his black-framed glasses. The Bishop sent him with a special purpose to St Mary's Parish in 1952. The costs for constructing St. Mary's Hall were bankrupting the Parish. His mission was to retire that debt.

They built the Hall next to the Church and Rectory. It filled the need for a gym for the nearby school and a place for church meetings. This building project had cost much more than the church leadership expected. After a few years floundering with the bills, the Bishop assigned Father O'Brien to the parish, replacing Father Donavon. First among Father O'Brien's duties was to be the parish priest, but the high second priority was to use his skills and mastery of fundraisers to retire the huge hall debt. Father, a term never attributed to our dads, ran the parish and was the final word on everything. Father O'Brien was the central power in the parish and somewhat mysterious to us kids. If there was one person we dared not to mess with, it was Father.

We never saw him wearing anything but his black shoes, black slacks and a black shirt with the white Roman collar. No one in our little part of the world had more respect and influence than Father O'Brien.

Nobody dared even a slight joke at his expense, and that included the adults. He could dictate whatever he felt was correct for the church, his decisions were final, and no good Catholics would ever think of challenging his authority. Our belief was that God anointed him to be His spokesman on earth to our little parish.

Like all priests, Father O'Brien attended the seminary and studied the gospels and teachings of the Church for twelve years. After taking the required 1-year sabbatical at the end of his studies, the Bishop ordained him to lead a parish. All the great mystical symbols of the Faith: the gold chalice & ciborium, the Eucharist, the incense, the confessional, the high Altar, the black cassocks, and the Roman collar were his and his alone. Only he could perform the great miracle of the Mass and that power gave him unquestioned authority over all in the church. His celibacy made him purity personified and a spiritual force unlike anyone else. We both loved and feared him. The affection and respect he commanded never wavered, even during the rare times life exposed his human imperfections.

Father Ralph O'Brien was, like many priests, an alcoholic. His temper was quick and hot and his drinking must have helped it flash. All except the newest and the youngest altar boys were in dread of Father's explosive disposition. None of us wanted to be the object of Father's wrath if we somehow screwed up the sanctity of one of the seven sacraments. Parents would never question Father O'Brien if he berated their son; It wasn't like he was a little league umpire making a bad call who would suffer the backlash from the boy's parents. Sometimes he acted like a two ulcer man working a three ulcer job.

Every once in a while, some poor sap of an altar boy who wasn't able to keep the reverence or concentration during Mass would commit some gaff. As a result, he became Father O'Brien's personal scapegoat. Any slight infraction of the altar boy etiquette and Father might explode during Mass, right out there in front of God and everybody. Father would give the offender a good scolding, right out loud calling the unfortunate altar boy a "little pot licker" in a loud and most scathing tone of voice. That label meant that the offending altar boy was a lost soul, there was no reasonable hope of redemption, he was to be a pot licker for life.

The nuns would choose some trustworthy boys to run special errands during school hours. It was frequent that a student would forget and leave an item like a book or a glove in Church from the morning Mass. Other times the Sisters might want an educational aid like a candle, or cruets, or some other item brought over from the church. In such a case the sisters at school would send one or two boys off to the Church to retrieve the item. On one of those days they sent Mark and Nocks.

Back in the 1960s and before, St. Mary's Church doors always were unlocked, so going into the Church was easy. People came into St. Mary's at all hours for solitary prayers, bring or refresh flowers, light candles, or even dust the place a bit. As Mark and Nocks entered the Church on their errand, Father O'Brien was in the Church, but he didn't realize the boys were there with him. Mark whispered to Nocks, "Be quiet Nocks, let's see what he's doing." Hidden from view at the back of the Church, as quiet as they could be, they watched Father with intense interest.

Even though Father thought he was in an empty church, he crossed the front altar and genuflected with his usual deep religious panache. He paused for a fraction of a second when his knee touched the floor and bowed his head reverently. Before he rose, he made a careful sign of the cross. First his right-hand fingers went to his forehead, then to his stomach. Next, he finished crossing his hands to his left, then to his right shoulders. It was the same worshipful genuflection he displayed for a Church full of worshipers at High Mass on Christmas Eve.

Mark and Nocks reported what they saw to their playmates at the next recess. "I couldn't believe Father!" Mark reported to the gang and continued, "It was just like he thought the Church was full. He acted the same. He didn't know anyone was watching. It was all for God."

Because of who he was, we were very interested in

Father O'Brien. Everyone hushed up and listened to Mark and Guz's description of Father's pious gestures in the solitude of an empty church. It was awe-inspiring to us kids. Nothing could bring home the reality of the Church's teachings more than observing these pure and sincere demonstrations of humility Father made in the servitude of God in a vacant Church.

Father's faith was always on display. When he said Mass, he would never crack a smile or show any expression. His demeanor exposed his total devotion and reverence, except for the occasional flash of white-hot anger directed at an offender of proper Mass decorum. Anyone, altar boy, nun, or a parishioner who interrupted or distracted from the serious and holy nature of the Mass would get a swift reprimand. Father expected every man, woman, and child respect the Mass. It was the most important experience in our universe.

Father's incredible intensity grew during his saying of a Mass and climaxed when he came to performing the sacrament of the Holy Eucharist. By that time in the service, he'd have beads of sweat dripping off his coal black hair on the back of his head. He'd be so wet it was almost as if he just stepped out of the shower. He had that same passion during a Midnight Mass on Christmas Eve with a packed Church full of parishioners and guests as he did at a 6am Saturday morning services in August for a handful of poor Spanish-speaking farm migrants. Father left no doubt in anyone's mind that he believed God empowered him. God chose him to perform the miracle of turning water and wine into the actual body and blood of Jesus. Father's conduct of the Mass was both faith-affirming to us Believers and at the least, mesmerizing to everyone else there in attendance at the old red brick church on the North side of town.

As Nocks later told it, even at the tender age of 8 years the rookie Altar Boys realized Father O'Brien's power and passion. But with their new special access to him they found out what a wonderful warm man he was too. When Sister took the altar boy recruits to the Rectory office and announced them to Father, he was studying some correspondence at his messy old oak roll-top desk. It was like he was a different person from the high-strung priest that they saw every day at Mass. He greeted us with a friendly smile, his teeth so white his smile seemed to explode on his face. He welcomed us in a most soothing deep voice, "Your being handpicked to become altar boys is a very great honor. You'll need good trainers and so I'm assigning you to two of the best altar boys I've ever had." He nodded toward the other side of the room. Two older boys were observing our conversation with Father from Father's well-worn burgundy leather couch. The boys were Steve Doyle and David Donahue, two 5th graders who were like movie stars in the eyes of us little guys.

Steve was a serious person and a very good student. He was tall and thin with blond short-cropped hair.

He carried himself with a grace and panache. Steve always conducted himself with a reserved demeanor when serving Mass. He was distant from the rest of us, likeable, but a loner.

Dave was his complete opposite, short and dumpy, he had long brown unkempt hair and dark horn-rimmed glasses. He was affable and outgoing, quick with a giggle. Dave's body language was casual when he served Mass. He moved around the altar looking as if he'd just thrown a strike at the bowling alley. But although it wasn't easy to see, Dave was just as serious about Mass as Steve. They were great altar boys and were Father O'Brien's favorites.

Father reached down and let out a small grunt as he pulled on an old squeaky desk drawer. He stirred around in the drawer and came up with three folded white cards. He gave them to us new recruits. The cards were the Mass prayers, all in Latin, that every altar boy memorized before serving their first Mass. "It's important that you memorize these prayers inside out," he said, "because you must recite these prayers out loud during the Mass, without the cards".

The red printed prayers on the cards were the Priest's, the altar boy prayers in black. Father watched us boys looking over the prayer cards and could see the intimidation on our faces. It was a lot of memorization. He'd seen that same look on previous recruit's faces before and he re-assured us, "For your first week as servers you can read off the cards at

Mass but after that you must say them by heart. It looks hard at first, but I know you'll catch on fast." he said, and the newest altar boy trainees looked at each other and nodded in the affirmative. "Do you have questions?", He asked. Again, we boys glanced at each other.

Nice as he was, Father intimidated all three of us. We couldn't talk. Father knew we were uncomfortable, and he smiled, let out a little chuckle as he stood up from his cluttered desk and said, "Then kneel for my special blessing."

We complied and Father made the sign of the cross over each of us. He laid his big soft hands on each of our heads, all the time saying a rhythmic Latin prayer. He finished the prayer and turned us over to our new mentors, Steve and Dave, saying to them, "Take these excellent young altar boy candidates over to the Church, find them a good fitting cassock and surplice, and start their training. I can tell they will be great altar boys". Steve and Dave jumped to their feet and took us three altar boy prospects across the small yard from the Rectory over to the Church.

The Church has two sacristies upfront. Each one is behind the two minor altars on either side of the center altar. The priest's on the right side. A smaller sacristy for altar boys is on the left. The boy's side has an extra entrance going into the Church's nave. Steve and Dave took the three of us through the nave and for the first time, into the altar boy's sacristy.

The Women's Altar Society kept the closets inside the boy's sacristy full of black cassocks and fine white linen surplices. All the cassocks were long-sleeved with high collars in assorted sizes to accommodate all the altar boys from the third to the twelfth grades. On two special days, Christmas and Easter, altar boys wore red cassocks. With the black or the red, over each they wore the white surplus. A surplus is square necked half-sleeved, waist length frock-like linen garment. The ladies of the Altar Society kept each surplice ready for Mass. The creases on the pleats were razor sharp, each one starched and ironed to perfection.

From the sacristy, Steve and Dave began our instructions by telling us that the rules allowed for talking in the sacristy, but only in a low voice. We didn't know of this perk since everywhere else in the Church the only voices allowed were those being used in prayer or song. The sacristy had a mix of special "church only" smells from the spare white altar candles, the incenses and quick lighting charcoal briquettes used at funerals and Lenten services.

The sacristy and the altars were male bastions. Mothers, sisters, even the Dominican Nuns could not come into this sacred place once services started. All territory north of the communion rail was off limits to all women and girls. The church was a male protectorate and even as 8-year-old boys; we knew the Church favored boys over girls. In our first time inside the sacristy, we nosed around and explored our new domain. We tried on the black cassocks and white surpluses for the first time and admired our new "holy" look in the sacristy mirror.

The older boys would take us to the Church each day after school to practice serving Mass and reciting the Latin prayers. Steve and Dave showed a lot of patience with our slow learning. They took us through our duties during the Mass. Dave would laugh out loud at a dumb question or be quick with a joke when explaining the nuances of being an altar boy to the new recruits, something Steve never did. Steve was always serious, but he made sure we knew what expectations we needed to meet. Steve and Dave's futures were on the same trajectory, the older boys we liked so much both grew up and became priests.

We had so many details to learn before they allowed us to serve Mass. Steve and Dave taught the proper way to light the candles (start at the lowest furthest from the tabernacle in the center of the altar, right to left). The proper way to stand (no slouching). How to kneel (no slouching here either). The way to fold hands (palms and fingers together with the thumbs crossed). How to ring the bells (sometimes a single ring, other times three distinct rings). They showed us how to fold the cloth on the communion rail (two-person job with a procession to the center of the rail and one sharp right angle marked to the end of the altar). These future priests taught us how to pour the holy water and how to hold the bowl just right for

Father when he washed his fingers to prepare for communion. They taught the proper way to pour the water and wine into the sacred gold chalice both before and after Father O'Brien performed the great miracle of turning the wine and simple wafer of bread into the literal Body and Blood of Jesus Christ.

Whenever crossing in front of the high altar, they taught their new recruits to pause and genuflect, right knee all the way to the floor, moving down and up together as one. The message we got was to act serious. This was no place for our misbehavior. They told us, and we believed it, that God selected us through His personal representative, i.e. the Parish Priest, to assist performing the miracle of the Mass.

Boys never complained about being selected to serve mass because it was such a high honor to be an altar boy. At the same time, no one ever said they enjoyed serving Mass either. We served Saturday's Mass, which started at 7am all year. During the school year, Sunday Mass began at 8am and 10am. Summer daily Mass began at 7am weekdays and Saturdays (and summers rarely had over three people attend), Sunday Mass was at 7am, 9am, and 11am with a 7pm Mass for the Migrant Workers. Whenever a Funeral, wedding, and the special Lenten Services occurred, Father recruited extra altar boys.

The Penguins made sure all altar boys possessed a mimeographed six-week schedule that they sent through the mail. No one ever just quit or didn't show up as scheduled. When Father deemed someone a good altar boy or, better yet, priest material, the more Mass they served. Dave Donahue, Steve Doyle, and the 8-year-old rookies, Mark Monoly, Dick Gusnoki, carried the load for years. They served far more Masses and special services than any of the other couple of dozen altar boys.

They expected altar boys to take communion when serving all Masses, including school days. Catholic rules required fasting for three hours before having communion. That rule allowed for servers and kids who took the sacrament to pack a breakfast and bring it to school. Communion takers ate at the start of the first morning class. Mark Monoly and Nocks Gusnocki were two of the few kids that took communion every day Mass served or not. No matter how long they took, or how noisy or messy they were, the Penguins never said a word to any communion taking kid while they ate at their desks. Instead, there was an encouragement and approval for their having taken this most holy sacrament.

"It doesn't sound like fun being an Altar Boy." Molly said as she shifted the Jeep into high gear and headed us east into the morning sun. I answered, "I wouldn't describe it as fun, but it gave us a sense of duty and self-worth."

"It's like they intimidated and scared you boys into doing it," she continued. "There's a bit of truth to that Molly," I replied, "That's how any organization indoctrinates youngsters. There's fear, symbolism, rituals, authority figures, but we also had to learn discipline, confidence, and how to be reliable. More importantly for me, being an altar boy is how I became best of friends with Mark and The Nocks."

I told her that even though Mark was one of the superb kids and students; he had a mischievous side too. As an altar boy, he was reliable and respectful, but he'd be quick to give you the crossed eyes to get you to laugh during any part of Mass. During dual genuflections, Mark might give you a little nudge, not to knock you over, that would have been too much. He'd bump you just enough to have you lurch to regain your balance. As we got older, if you were serving Mass and he was in the congregation, he would wait until Father O'Brien looked the other way. Then Mark would itch his nose with his middle finger and smirk. He was quick to help you with any chore to get you to the baseball field or playground faster. Mark became everyone's best friend, well-liked by every parent and all our teachers. As he grew older, he became tall and handsome. The girls considered him a heartthrob.

Nocks was one of the few non-Irish kids in town. The only Polish kid in school, we Irish kids loved to good-naturedly tease him about being a Pollock. He'd give it right back, never backing down from his proud Polish heritage. Gusnocki lived in a perpetual state of dishevelment, normally wearing wrinkled shirts, his brown hair long and usually not well combed. Nocks had the big black horn-rimmed glasses and a look of pouty puzzlement about him. But he was quick-witted and street smart.

His parents, long time "Carneys", ran a food truck in the summer traveling with their rigs and campers to festivals and county fairs, or as they called them, the "shows". He would disappear every summer with his family and then come back to school each fall with great stories about all the cities and "shows" he'd been to during the season. The Gusnocki family lived hand-to-mouth, they didn't earn much more that survival income. Even us naïve kids saw that they didn't have much of anything, but none of us cared about his parent's income status. Nocks was a buddy who backed you up no matter what. He was loyalty personified, and he got back more than he gave.

One winter day out on the schoolyard during 6th grade recess Nocks threw a snowball at a buddy that flew off target and despite Mark's warning to "look out", hit our teacher, Sister Roberta. To make matters worse, the snowball hit her square in the side of her habit. Her habit flew off and exposed her bare head to every kid on the school grounds. Sister's reaction wouldn't have been any different had her clothes blown off and left her naked in front of us. Her modesty compromised, she scrambled to the ground red-faced to pick up her habit and placed it back on her head. Then the fun began.

Nocks disappeared around the corner of the school to

hide as the nuns started looking for the guilty snowball thrower. After recess and back in our classroom, Sister Roberta started grilling us to find out who threw the snowball. No matter what she said or how much she threatened to punish us all, she failed to get anyone to admit being or seeing the culprit.

Then the big gun came. A visibly angry Sister Thomas Anne, the principal of the school, came into our classroom demanding that the guilty party confess. "Right now!" She demanded in a hostile tone of voice, "I want the person who threw that snowball to have the courage to admit it".

Nocks wanted to admit to the deed but kept silent when he saw Mark looking to him, pressing his finger to his lips to encourage silence. Every student in the classroom knew Nocks was the guilty party, but no one would ever rat out Nocks. Sister Thomas Anne's intimidation tactics failed. No one pointed a finger at Nocks.

Father appointed her the principal for good reasons; "TA" as we called her, understood us misbehaving kids. TA turned the screws tighter saying in a stern voice, "Mr. Monoly, you warned Sister Roberta. That means you saw the person who threw the snowball. Who threw it Mark?".

Mark stood up and replied without hesitation. "I saw

who threw it. But Sister, I don't tattle on my friends."
Sister bit her bottom lip and took a deep breath to
display her displeasure. Casting a slow eye at every
kid in the class, she said the worst thing any Catholic
school kid could ever hear. "Well then, Mark, I
suppose you need to walk yourself over to the rectory.
Chat with Father O'Brien about this secret of yours
and see what he thinks." Mark looked stunned but
still, he refused to identify Nocks. He even gave
Nocks a side glance and a wink to signal him to
continue to hold his silence. Mark got out of his seat
and headed out the classroom door to make his sorry
way over to the rectory. Mark spent two long hours
with Father O'Brien.

It seemed like Mark might never come back from the
Rectory when, later that day while Sister Roberta was
at the chalkboard showing us how to diagram
sentences, all the students jumped to their feet.
Father O'Brien, accompanied by Mark, burst into the
classroom. "Please take your seats," Father said and
motioned Mark to stand with him at the front of the
class. "Sister, may Mark and I chat with your class for
a few minutes?" Sister Roberta nodded in agreement,
as if she had a choice. Father gave a gentle pat to
Mark's back and said, "Go ahead, Mr. Monoly."

In a clear and steady voice, Mark began by saying, "I
asked Father if he'd hear my confession a few
minutes ago and he agreed. I told him everything that
happened on the playground and I told him if he
wanted to tell you anything I confessed, I'm OK with

him telling you. But he said he can't do that, that what I told him is between him, me, and God. So, I want to tell Sister something", and he turned to Sister and said "I still won't tell on my friend, but I will tell you he didn't mean it. It was an accident that you got hit with a snowball. Father tells me that makes a big difference and you need to be told that nobody intentionally threw at you. Honestly Sister, my friend aimed at someone else and it just missed them and hit you instead."

Father O'Brien smiled and gave a knowing pat on Mark's back and said, "Thank you, Mark, you can take your seat now." Then he let out a loud sigh. He stared down at the floor. He took a minute to collect his thoughts, and the class waited. We thought we all might be on our way straight to hell.

It seemed like forever before he looked up at the class and began, "Mr. Monoly told you he took confession. I can't tell you that myself because I made certain promises to God a long time ago. With these vows I promised Him that when a person comes to confession, I would, like all priests, not ever say anything to anyone else about the person who goes into the confessional or what they said in that confession.

There's a good reason for that. When you have a problem or have a sin to confess, you can come talk to me. No third party can know what transpired. These are the rules. No one else will ever know what we say in confession, everything said is between you, me, and God. The best part is, if you are truly sorry for the sins you've committed, God will always forgive you."

Mark had played Father O'Brien pretty well by confessing. But Father's wisdom prevailed. He gave Mark a penance of his telling Sister that the snowballing occurred without malice. That gave Father the wiggle room to discuss the incident without breaking the confidence of the confessional. "As Mark just said a few minutes ago to everyone, he has a friend who, with no intent, caused someone some pain. Here Sister Roberta, a total innocent, suffered injury. But that's not all. This incident is embarrassing for her. I'm glad Mark has disclosed to Sister that her getting hit with the snowball was not intentional. That helps put the whole story into the proper perspective.

We all admire loyalty; it is a noble quality to have. I join you all in your admiration of Mark for his loyalty to his buddy. I suspect many, if not all of you, are aware who our snowballer is and are withholding this information from Sister. You may consider yourself as a protector of one of your cronies. You may see yourself as saving him from some unjust punishment, and if that is your motive, it's a noble quality and I have nothing but admiration for those who stand by their pals. God admires those noble traits in you too, and that is of the greatest importance.

But my children, as you grow up and think about this

incident, you'll see how complicated everything in life can get. This little snowball caused pain. We don't want injustice to come of it. We want to do the right thing.

Deciding what the right thing to do in simple incidents sometimes gets complicated. You must determine right from wrong, it's not always easy to decide. Let me ask you, did you feel good protecting a friend or are you uncomfortable from the guilt of not telling the truth to our innocent victim Sister Roberta? And our snowball thrower, does he feel bad because his actions implicate everyone? I suspect so. Imagine how bad it must be for this culprit to see Mark get singled out and sent to the rectory... not too many live to tell about that now do they?", he said with a smile and a chuckle, and the class broke its collective silence and joined Father with loud giggles.

"Doing the right thing is hard. It can get harder and harder as you grow up in this complicated world. I hope today is a good lesson for us to consider the pain of the innocent. We need to think what God wants us to do. There is no doubt He wants us to take away the pain caused from the incident. Mark is a good role model. He sought help to find the right answers. He included God in helping him make his choice of action. God will show you the way like he did for Mark. Never forget God, take him with you on your journey. He'll always be there for you."

Father looked over at Sister Roberta and said "Sister,

I think we should let our snowball thrower off the hook, what do you say?" Sister replied with a smile "I agree Father, I thought someone threw at me on purpose, and that hurt the most. I feel better knowing it was an accident."

The Nocks rose to his feet. Later he said he thought we all heard his knees knocking in fear. He overcame his anxiety and confessed in a strong, confident, yet repentant voice "Sister, I threw the snowball, but just like Mark said, I missed the guy I threw at, I didn't mean to hit you, then I didn't know what to do. Then things started rolling; it's amazing to me how nobody told on me."

Then Nocks turned to Father O'Brien and said "Father, I'm sorry but I don't feel guilty, instead I appreciate having friends like these. I'm the luckiest guy in the world. All my friends, everyone in this class, and my best buddy Mark all stood quiet for me. I don't know what I've done to deserve such great friends." Nocks turned once again back to Sister and said in a sincere voice, "I'm sorry Sister for not speaking up sooner, but these guys got me all tongue-tied."

"I forgive you Richard", Sister said as she started wagging her finger menacingly at the Nocks, but then in a teasing tone of voice she said, "I'm glad you've come forward, and you're smart to wait a bit for me to cool down a bit. Believe me, I had some painful punishments in store for the snowballer. I mean pain with a capital P!" Everyone in the classroom laughed knowing full well she meant it.

"I think we've got this behind us now, but before I head back to the rectory, everyone please kneel for a blessing," Father said.   Everyone, including Sister Ann, got down on their knees, folded their hands, and with respect, bowed their heads as Father O'Brien made the sign of the cross over all of us. Father gave his blessing, "May God bless you all and may He continue to nourish these seeds of integrity that we've seen today in these fine children.  We pray that they find their way to show merciful justice and compassion for those in pain.  May God guide you. Lord, please be with us on our search for what is right.  Please guide us here in our small classroom, or when the world's larger issues like the growing war in Vietnam call us to be wise and just.  Last item Lord, can you please improve Mr. Gusnocki's aim when he throws a snowball?"  How could we not love Father O'Brien?

## Chapter 2 *Halloween and Continuing Catholic Development*

This day young Molly defies her tendencies for teenage volatility. She's in a good mood and drives our little red Jeep Wrangler with unwarranted confidence into the warm morning sun. The West Michigan side roads take us through the rolling hills, the last vestiges of the ancient sand dunes we are leaving behind us. Today, Molly is driving like a pro. She keeps the Jeep between the lines on the road. Not once does she slip off the pavement. The further we go, the more I can relax. The tension in my chest dissipates and the long drive becomes enjoyable.

Molly's a great conversational strategist. This day she uses her considerable skills to engage me on a comfortable topic. Then she keeps me chatting along to entertain her for the entire trip. The topic for her inquiry is my childhood.

I wonder if she knows we parents have an occasional compulsion to impart our personal history. We have stories we think are important. We all have certain events we lived through we think are important to leave for following generations. A bit of history about the family roots, or events we experienced that shaped our values, things worth remembering.

She gets the conversation rolling with a question/statement. "I can't understand how growing up in a strict Catholic family differs much from the way you and Mom have raised us kids."

She doesn't know how difficult the question is that she's asking. I consider my answer for a few minutes. I grew up in the 60s, a conflicting experience for my generation. It may be hard to explain, but my childhood was different, perhaps even unique. It's worth remembering and sharing. Molly notices my slow response; she knows it means that I have a considered answer.

I begin by saying, "My parents raised me as a Catholic, in a Catholic school. We were a respectful Catholic family. This upbringing had a huge impact on me, my friends, and my perceptions in a world that seemed to spin a new crisis every day.

The 1960s gave everyone an electric shock. For example, no one alive had ever experienced a president being assassinated. As Catholics, that special bond we had for having the first Catholic Presidency end in murder was devastating beyond words. The shock assassinations didn't end with JFK. His brother Bobby Kennedy and Reverend Martin Luther King, men we looked up to as peacemakers, were both killed in cold blood. The violence unprecedented, their murders beyond shocking."

Race riots disturbed our society. Almost every large city in America broke out in flames when angry crowds turned to arson. The words "Burn Baby Burn" rose from the streets amplified by the largest venue in our culture, the televised evening news. Leaders from every segment of society warned we were spinning into anarchy.

The full undercurrent pushing all the chaos washing over us was the War in Vietnam. Disorder, disobedience, and near outright rebellion blasted into our homes through the new medium of TV. No one could escape being affected by what we saw every night as we huddled up to watch the half hour evening news shows.

My upbringing should have been that of an uncomplicated farm town kid. My small group of friends and I grew up Catholic. As Catholics, our families taught us to define the world from a strong base of the Catholic values. Our parents raised us in the same strong traditions, same as their parents and grandparents. But they don't call it the tumultuous 60s for the lack of reasons. The youth of my generation became rebellious, we challenged everything, including the sacred teachings of the Church.

For two thousand years, the culture of the Church and its institutions dominated the thoughts and morals of most Catholics. But I'm not sure even the Church made it through the 60s unchanged. I'm not sure if the Church became a catalyst for resistance to the War, or like everything else, became another institution dominated by the War in Vietnam. The war changed everyone and everything.

By the time I became a senior in high school every day included seeing, hearing, discussing, feeling, or reading about the war in Vietnam. Every day it seemed to get worse. College students and other young people even bombed buildings here in America to shock the nation into getting out of Vietnam. Black Panthers armed themselves as protection from "The White Devils." President Nixon lied about Vietnam and just about everything else. Overt messages for rebellion and counter culture permeated our music. Drug usage, not yet reaching into small town high schools, fueled emotions even higher. Young men went on TV and burnt their draft cards, a criminal offense, to demonstrate their complete resistance to the war. Many others fled to Canada to avoid being forcibly drafted into the armed services. The culture produced slogans like "don't trust anyone over 30," and "Tune in, turn on, and drop out."

As we grew up, fear was our everyday companion. As far back as I can remember, we elementary students felt the very real threat of atomic bombs targeting us. Even in our small rural town surrounded by corn and bean fields, the terror of nuclear war touched us. It existed like an impending thunderstorm swirling around us. It dominated our childhoods, even in places like our little farm town of Carson City."

Carson City, Michigan remains as it always has, a quiet rural village of about 1000 persons in the "middle of the Mitten." Most of the houses are two stories tall, wood framed, and built on "Michigan basements," homes built with field stones brought in from the farms and used for the foundations. Other than farming, the major industries are in healthcare and energy. Carson City Hospital with 30 beds being the largest employer in town and Carson City Refinery employing about 20 people. The city has a one block central business district with 2 family restaurants, 3 bars, a pharmacy, a hardware store, two small grocery stores, and 5 gas stations. People who can't find a scarce job in town commute to work in larger nearby towns. A few residents drove 80 miles round trip each day to work in the automobile plants in Lansing, the state capital. Founded in 1868, Carson City is a placid middle-class rural community surrounded by family farms.

Most of Carson's Catholic parents earned their high school diplomas from St. Mary's Academy. A dinky country school, it graduated as few as 4 students in 1912. The largest class in 1938 graduated 12 students. Baby Boomers made up my class of 1970, the largest class ever with a whopping 30 students. Each year as we progressed to the next grade, the Dominican Sisters at St. Mary's had no choice but to reconfigure the school's small classrooms. It wasn't easy but somehow, they squeezed our big group into the small classrooms every year.

"My class of 1970 grew up at the start of the rapid demise of small-town parochial schools.  St. Mary's Academy, like all parochial schools in Michigan, suffered a financial mortal blow in the mid-1960s.  It happened when the voters rescinded Parochial-Aide, a state funding of education in private schools.  Our high school became a casualty from the lack of state funding, closing in 1966.  The elementary and grade schools hung on a little longer, but closed a few years after the high school closed.

We 30 boys and girls of the class of 1970 finished the 8th grade in the venerable old Catholic school.  Much to the chagrin of our parents, we started high school at Carson City Crystal Area Public schools.  The nearby public high school was next to Saint Mary's Academy, a mere 200 yards down a gentle treeless slope to the south.  We weren't strangers to the public school.  We'd been in the building many times and knew it well.

Because we grew up in a small town, we Catholic kids interacted with all the students and teachers before attending any of the classes. We were no surprise to them either.  As we started our public education, we found our science skills a little lacking.  But in every other subject, we discovered how superior a Catholic education was to the public-school systems. Individual exceptions existed but overall, the public-school kids didn't match up academically with us Catholic kids. We still attended the daily morning Mass. The public school was close by, a short block away from St. Mary's Church.

The most significant academic change for us entering the public-school system was the lack of catechism classes. To meet that need, the diocese of Grand Rapids instructed the parish to offer Continuing Catholic Development, or CCD, as we called it. The teachers for CCD came from a few clergy joined by devout parishioners. Each volunteer parishioner was hand-picked by Father O'Brien.

The weekly sessions replaced the earlier daily structured Catechism lessons. Including leaders from the parish was new, but the bishop's resources had changed. Now there were fewer and fewer women entering the convents. For years St. Mary's had at least a dozen Dominicans to teach us kids. When our class reached high school, only two nuns remained in the parish.

Every Monday night during the school year, they invited all the Catholic high school students to CCD. We met at the Dominican Convent for an evening of religious instruction. Mark Monoly, Brenna Brennan, Darby Donahue, The Nocks, and I never missed a session. We were the most dependable attendees. The rest of the Catholic students' attendance fluctuated each week.

CCD sessions started and ended with a group prayer. The content featured programs on Catholicism and how our Faith and the Church should be the center of our daily life. The sessions provoked lively discussions, all very freewheeling. A few times the discussions were hot and emotional. But the rules for classes required that everyone to show respect for those with differing opinions.

Because we had so many students in the class of 1970, we didn't get a lay instructor. Instead, they blessed us by assigning us to one of the two available Dominican nuns. Sister Ann, in her black and white habit and flowing robes, led and monitored the discussions in her always soft tender voice. Sometimes she'd have an 8mm film or a filmstrip sent from the Diocese.

The filmstrips came with a vinyl record that required an operator to synchronize the sound to the film strip. These black vinyl albums would signal to whoever of us students ran the filmstrip projector that night, when to advance it. A slight gong sound to on the record gave the signal. Nothing delighted the group more than being able to make an exaggerated fuss at one of our operator friends when they missed the gong signal. Taunting the offender became our group's favorite blood sport.

The purpose of the filmstrips was to provoke discussion. After a showing, we'd all pull our chairs into a circle for a "rap session" in the small family room of the convent. The Convent was a small white two-story house, kitty corner across the street from the rectory. It wasn't anything like the other church buildings because it once had been a private home. Painted white, the modest wood building was a contrast to the solid red brick of the Church, Rectory, Hall, and School. It sat across the street from all the other church buildings. In a residential neighborhood, it seemed less official, important, and prominent than the other Church buildings. The Convent's placement seemed to re-enforce the Church's doctrine that treated women as less important than men. As we grew older and matured, we came to challenge this culture of female subservience.

As we grew into young men and women, no Catholic kids had thoughts about dating each other. The Catholic girls were the smartest and cutest in the school district but none of us Catholic Boys ever dated one of them. The upbringing of the Church and perhaps the CCD discussions brought us together like a family, more than we realized. A romance between us Catholic kids, for whatever the reasons, not only never happened, none of us had conscious thoughts about dating "in-Church."

The prettiest girl in school, not an easy competition, had to be Brenna Brennan. Brenna had short dark hair and beautiful big round brown eyes any boy could get lost in. She lit up every room she entered when she flashed her effervescent smile.  Brenna's gentle nature and kindness gave her a direct and sincere connection with everyone.  Her dad was Dr. Brennan.

He'd come to town in the late 1930s and founded Carson City Refinery.  Brenna wanted acceptance for being her own person.  She didn't enjoy living in the shadow of her dad.  But because of her father's high status in the community, she never cracked into the inner circle of friends.  She couldn't become middle class like the rest of us.  We came into the world as sons and daughters of factory workers, farmers, and middle-class shopkeepers.  Every once in a while, one of us would call her "rich," something she'd vehemently deny.  But compared to the rest of us, yeah, she was rich.

Brenna had a sweet and unsophisticated manner about her.  Those qualities often made her a target for school pranks and put-ons.  Those incidents never intended to be cruel because we all liked Brenna.  She got average to good grades, but she didn't match her father's intellect.  Brenna never figured out how to disarm the rest of us from what we saw as her lofty status.  Her parent's wealth created a barrier between her and the rest of us.

Dr. Brennan built the only ranch style home in Carson City.  It is on the south side of town on a huge 40-acre lot.  The house is on a small rise at the end of a private long winding paved road.  The road runs over a small private bridge to cross a small ravine.  They

45

made the stately house from grey bricks and it's the only home in town with a swimming pool. Brenna's home rose above that ravine, setting it physically apart from the city. In fact, the driveway ran out past the city limits. The house subtly underscored her family's wealth.

Dr. Brennan drove the only Cadillac in town, a bright blue Eldorado, and he bought Brenna got a brand-new 1969 Red Camaro for her 16th birthday. Those status symbols were way above the norm for our community. No one else in Carson City could afford a Cadillac or had the money to buy a brand-new car for any of their teenagers.

The community loved and respected Dr. and Mrs. Brennan, but Catholics held them at arm's length in the Church. This was his second marriage, his first ended in divorce long before he came to Carson City. Although he and Mrs. Brennan were members of the Church and steady attendees at Mass, Father O'Brien would not give them the sacraments. Doing so would violate Catholic doctrine. Divorce was a mortal sin in the eyes of the Church, and hell was the future for those not honoring their marriage vows to their literal graves. Dr. and Mrs. Brennan's marriage outside the Church lurked in the background of the relationships they had with the local Catholics. Their sin pre-empted their normalization, it was the spiritual separator between them and the rest of the parish.

Brenna's oldest sister became a nun in a cloistered

convent. This was about as hard core Catholic as it gets. She took the required vow of silence and no one, including the Brennan family, could have any contact with her, even at her wish.

These factors played on Brenna and as a result, she was shy and insecure. She was the object of many a prank because of her gullibility. No one doubted her unwavering good intentions. She was well like, but only a few Catholic kids allowed her to be a close friend.

All of us, except perhaps Brenna, knew her life would differ from the rest of ours. We all knew her wealthy doctor Refinery-owning father would take care of her financial needs through her college years and the rest of her life. The rest of us would have to scrape our way through school if we were ever to find high-paying jobs.

Dick Gusnocki, The Nocks, was another regular attender to CCD classes. He was the proud son of a Polish Carney and spent the summers traveling with his family to fairs and community celebrations around the Midwest. We knew Nocks for having the best relationship with his father than any other kid in town. Every Saturday Nocks would be off with his dad in his dad's step van for a day of running the dry cleaning, his dad's off-season job. He was always talking about he and his dad hanging out together and their family travels during the summer "shows." The rest of us kids struggled with our relationships with our dads in

47

our teen years. Nocks made us all envious of his great relationship with his dad.

Unlike the rest of us, Nock's future was clear and waiting for him. His destiny was to go into business with his dad as a carney, something he looked forward to without a thought of doing anything different. Everyone in the CCD group secretly wished they would have a similar destiny with their fathers too. But for the rest of us, our relationships with our fathers were lacking.

It was easy to find conflict with our parents, particularly with our fathers. Dads in the 1960s had their stay at home wives do the bulk of parenting. Most dads didn't spend a lot of time with their children. To further widen the gap as we got older, there was a cornucopia of subjects that caused conflict. The biggest was the war in Vietnam. We also had radical music, the civil rights movement, topics like zero population growth, pollution, abortion, women's liberation, fashion, the counterculture. All divisive topics and a bomb waiting to explode in every family.

Nocks and his dad would have conversations on volatile topics without conflict. They had the ability to communicate about any subject, no matter how serious the topic might be. Beyond being a father and son, they were friends.

Maybe his unique and close friendship with his dad was the basis of Nock's ability to be friends with everyone. The Nocks had more friends than anybody in school. His personality was an easy mix for integrating into any faction. He was the guy used as the model when they invented the word "affable". One of his personal qualities was his being just offbeat enough to bring out everyone's protective nature for him.

Most of us were born in Carson City but not Nocks. He and his family had moved from nearby Ionia when he was in fourth grade. There were a handful of other classmates born somewhere else. They never made it to 100% acceptance like Nocks did. By the time our senior year came the Nocks was about 5' 10" and a pudgy 180 lbs. He had dark brown hair with long bangs in front hanging over his black-framed glasses. Gusnocki had a tough guy pouty look about him like Elvis, but he wasn't one of the school toughs, not even close. The Nocks was Mr. Everybody. Everyone was always at ease with him.

We talked the Nocks into doing all kinds of mischievous acts. When whatever caper he joined or started went bad, the guy getting caught and held responsible inevitably would be the hapless Nocks. The best example of his uncanny ability to be saddled as the patsy in a teenage stunt was the time he got a group of classmates together for some misbehaving on Halloween night. Nocks was the chief conspirator of his "gang."  He loaded everyone into his dad's old beat up dry-cleaning step van and drove them off into the night on a mischief making mission.

After imbibing in some Boones Farm, the cheap but popular wine of the college and hippie set, the band of pranksters set out cruising the town.  Nocks was careful to watch out for the little ones out trick or treating. He drove down the side streets with a sharp eye out for the metal garbage cans residents set out for the next morning's garbage pickup day.  The city Father's hadn't considered moving garbage day, so residents set their garbage to the curb for the next morning's routine pickup. When no homeowners were watching, Nocks stopped the step van and dispatched the teenage villains who knocked over the trash and spread smelly garbage all over the backstreets.

Typical of the Nock's ill stared luck, the 2 local Carson City Police officers were observing the garbage can carnage.  It wasn't long before they pulled the step van over a block away from the Monoly home.  The chief of police, Glen Hughes, was behind the wheel and had followed the trail of garbage on the streets to Nock's step van.  He correctly assumed Halloween vandals were behind the messes and the trash spills in the wake of the Gusnocki step-van made it obvious.

Glen Hughes had been the homegrown chief of police at Carson City for 20 years.  Glen was a faithful Catholic, had graduated from St. Mary's academy, and knew everything about everyone and every family in town.  He was a big man, 6 ft. 4 inches tall, weighed a good 250 pounds, and was tough enough to tangle with Paul Bunyan.

He used to tease the high school boys to challenge him to impromptu wrestling matches whenever he was out of uniform at any school event or social gathering.  Every boy in town tried to wrestle Glen and found out he was more than they ever hoped to handle.  The Chief had macho swagger and always warned the boys if they "messed with the bull, they'd get the horn."  Despite his size and his undefeated wrestling record, he was a lovable, gentle giant and a good man.

Whenever the city budget afforded or when they received a special grant fund, the City would employ a deputy.  The budget of Carson City was in good shape in these years, and Glen had hired a deputy from the nearby town of Westphalia.  The young skinny police officer wannabe's name was Gerhard Schmidt.  Schmidt, all 5 feet 5 inches of him, qualified for police work by taking the minimum required law enforcement classes at Lansing Community College. He earned a reputation for being an inflexible hard ass trying to make a name for himself.

Carsonites gave Schmidt the nickname "Barney," as was their habit to give this nickname to all of Glen's deputies.  The moniker "Barney," came from the Andy Griffith Show.  An actor named Don Knotts played a bumbling idiotic deputy named Barney Fife.  As we grew up, a lot of us kids thought "Barney" was a synonym for the word "deputy."

Chief Glen Hughes walked up to the driver's side of the step van while Barney Fife stood near the doors at the rear. The police cruiser's glaring spotlight cut into the darkness, illuminating the grey, rusty, step van. Glen, knowing every kid in the van, instructed Nocks to step out. The chief greeted him with a happy sing-song voice. "Well, Happy Halloween Mr. Gusnocki. I hope you are driving safely tonight." The Nocks replied with a sincere smile, "Good evening Chief, it sure is a pleasant evening isn't it sir?" Glen smiled right back and played the game to checkmate, "Your vehicle appears to be spilling garbage out its back-end Mr. Gusnocki. Everywhere you've been tonight there is a trail of garbage all over the roads. Might we have a little peek into the back of your van and see what the problem is?"

Glens question was all it took, the doors on back of van flew open and before Barney Fife reacted, every boy and girl in the van came flying out. The band of teenagers in the step-van pulled the old run-like-crazy-in-every-other-direction routine. They bolted from the step van, escaping the flat-footed Barney, and regrouping as planned, unannounced, at the back door of the Monoly house a few blocks up the street.

Glen stood in the road with his arms crossed, rocking back and forth on his heels. He continued his mocking of Nocks saying, "My goodness Mr. Gusnocki, seems you had quite a party going on in your dad's van, this is your dad's van now isn't it?" Nocks smiled sheepishly knowing Glen was about to give him some small-town justice. "Yes Sir Chief, it is." "Now I suppose your dad wouldn't approve of his son making messes all over town, now would he?" Nocks reluctantly nodded in the affirmative.

"If your dad knew you were out with your pals were also doing a little drinking on Halloween, maybe that Boones Farm I'm smelling on you, that's something your dad would frown upon now wouldn't he Mr. Gusnocki?" Nocks again meekly nodded his head in agreement. "Now Mr. Gusnocki I suspect if we give you the choice of me taking you home as my little trick or treat to share with your dad or, you volunteering to do a little community service, say a little street cleaning, I bet I can guess what you'd choose. I bet you'd want to go with the Carson City Police Force tonight rather than us giving you an escort to your home. Would I be correct that you'll want to ride with us                                              tonight?"
Nocks couldn't help but chuckle when he saw Glen holding back laughter, "It's quite a coincidence Chief, I was thinking about doing a little cleanup anyway, so joining you would be a pleasure." "Wonderful choice Mr. Gusnocki," Glen said laughing out loud and putting a friendly arm around Nock's shoulder. "Mr. Gusnocki, welcome to the inaugural Friends of the Carson City Police Halloween Trash Patrol."

Glen and Barney turned the police car spotlights onto

the first garbage mess in the road behind the step-van. "Go get em Mr. Gusnocki!" yelled Glen in a pleasant and encouraging tone of voice as the Nocks, knowing Glen and Barney owned his sorry butt for the rest of the night. Nock's only real choice was to grin and start picking up the trash in the streets.

A few houses away at the Monoly home, Mark was handing out Halloween candy to the treat or treaters ringing the front doorbell. Ma and Pa Monoly had kept him home Halloween night to preempt any mischief-making on his part. They knew full well Mark would join any of the many gangs of scoundrels out in force on Halloween night. Mrs. Monoly was in the kitchen when the back door burst open and about 20 kids came pouring into the house to hide from the cops. Brenna was at the head of the line and breathlessly burst out, "Uh, Happy Halloween Mrs. Monoly. We, uh, came over to see what Mark is doing tonight."

Everyone knew Mrs. Monoly was a bit of a stinker herself. She had no trouble seeing through the tommyrot. She said, wagging an accusing finger at Brenna, "Brenna Brennen, and you too Darby Donahue, I suspect since you've come bursting into my house tonight, you and your friends have been up to some mischief." "Ah well, Mrs. Monoly, let me tell you what happened. We were walking around talking and enjoying trick or treating when," and Mrs. Monoly cut her off, interrupting, "Brenna Brennen, how is it you think you can fool me on Halloween? I will ask you this and you better give me a truthful answer if you want my help. What have you and your little friends been doing tonight?" She said with a mock frown and a smirk.

Brenna couldn't fool Mrs. Monoly, but she tried her best. She replied with an earnest smile and sweetest tone of voice. "Mrs. Monoly, we came right here tonight and didn't do a thing to your house! But some of your neighbors may have their garbage cans tipped over and trash rolled all over the street." Mrs. Monoly, played along, seeing right through this story. But she tried but failed to hold back laughing out loud. Then, mimicking Breanna's voice said, "Ok, Breanna, I'm convinced you're incapable of monkey business. I know you didn't touch my garbage can. We put it in the garage tonight to keep it away from the likes of this group. All the same, I'll give you all Halloween amnesty. Go hide in the living room. Turn the off the lights. Chief Hughes is driving up and down the streets. He's looking for somebody, I suspect it's you guys." "Thank you, Mrs. Monoly," the gang of kids said in unison as they snuck into the Monoly darkened out living room. The lights off kept the police from noticing a crowd of teenagers hiding in the Monoly home.

"Hey Brenna," said Darby from behind the drapes from inside the Monoly darkened out living room. "Look, the police came by and they've got Nocks. They've stopped, got him out in front of the cop car and he's cleaning up the trash we've spread." From the darkened living room, Brenna and the others peeked out the window. Sure enough, there was Nocks, out in the street picking up the trash they spilled.

Darby asked, "Are you guys thinking what I'm thinking? We can take Nock's step van and go get some more garbage cans. What a hoot, Nocks will be picking it up." "Let's go!" came the unified answer. Mrs. Monoly tried to stop them, but the group hustled out the back door and disappeared into the night.

As soon as the police car passed by the Monoly home, the group back-tracked to the abandoned step-van. Nocks had taken the keys to the van with him, but his pals came up with a workaround. They started it by using the common knowledge farm town skill known as hot-wiring. Darby took over as the driver and soon they were back at the garbage can attacks. She kept the van a few blocks out ahead of the police car where The Nocks was busy cleaning up the back streets of Carson City.

One of the merry pranksters would hop out of the step van and knock over another garbage can. They'd jump back in and the van would move a couple more blocks ahead of the city cop car. The cops, with Nocks in their custody, would follow, Chief Hughes stopping the black and white at each mess, then sending the hapless Nocks out to pick up the trash, put it back in the garbage cans, and sweep the street. As soon as Nocks was out in the street picking up garbage, the step van would discharge another villain to upset yet another garbage can.

When Nocks was out front of the police car picking up trash, the young police deputy asked officer Glen why they hadn't arrested Nocks. Glen explained, "Look Gerhard, you take a good kid like this and send him to court, you can screw up his future. The judges up in the county seat don't aren't familiar with him or his family like we are. No doubt about it, Gusnocki's a good kid. Juvy court in Stanton would put him through the system and who knows what permanent damage might come to him there. This minor teenage offense might end up screwing his whole life up if we go by the book. Small town cops like us need to use discretion. We are the front line of small-town justice. When we use good judgement, we can prevent youthful mistakes like this from becoming life wrecking events.

Gusnocki's dad will call me in a day or two, or I'll see him in Church. There's no way he won't hear about this. He'll realize we put a little justice on young Mr. Gusnocki. At first he'll be hot, but he'll think through it and deal with his son rationally. If we'd taken him home tonight, the family might have resented us at some level. By having a little fun with young Gusnocki, they'll appreciate us. Trust me, this way our jobs will be easier down the line.

These kids, none of them are causing serious trouble. These farm boys will not become criminals. I've got a few men on the city council right now I've caught doing similar shenanigans when they were young. Young Gusnocki here knows we're screwing with him and he knows we're having a bit of fun at his expense. He and his friends are aware we've given them a break. We'll let them blow off a little steam. Let's hope it keeps them in our debt and helps prevent them from doing something with more serious consequences. He's one of the popular kids in school, who knows, maybe in a few years we'll be answering to a Mayor Nocks Gusnocki? Stranger things have happened."

So, they kept Nocks busy cleaning up garbage late into the night as the pattern of mischief continued, tip over, clean up, tip over, clean up, tip over.

No one knows who had the most fun that Halloween, the step-van vandals or Glen and Barney. The next day at school the Nocks took all the non-stop kidding with his typical good humor. But he vowed an undefined revenge on all those now known as the Step-Van Gang.

The local newspaper, "The Carson City Gazette", has a section in it named "Coming and Going." The column is for citizens to submit personal events in their lives. An example might be like, "Helen Flanagan received a letter from her lovely Aunt Tilly in Phoenix Arizona. She conveys Aunt Tilly's request to send greetings to all her friends in Carson City."

To make that Halloween night more memorable, someone using Brenna Brennan' s name submitted a "Coming and Going" article in the Gazette. It read, "We saw Richard Gusnocki coming and going as he volunteered to do city street cleaning last Halloween Night. Carson City's Finest Police Officers joined this heroic anti-vandal by keeping young Mr. Gusnocki and the sabotaged garbage cans illuminated during the cleanup. Go Nocks!"

Nocks gave every actor in the Halloween Step Van Caper the moniker of being a "Larry Cadodee." He never told any of us the full true meaning of what it meant to be a Larry Cadodee, but we knew it wasn't a compliment. Despite knowing it was a disparaging nickname used by Carney's, we delighted in being anointed with the byname. When he christened a "Larry Cadodee" it meant that person was on the Nock's list. Nocks cooked up a good-natured reprisal for every Halloween Larry Cadodee.

The Nock's Halloween retaliation campaign began with Brenna. She always denied being the author of the Coming and Going article in the local newspaper. The mention became a great source of amusement that autumn for our sleepy little town. His retaliation on her came within a week. He got her with his signature method of revenge, shaving cream. He surreptitiously filled her coat pockets, purse, hat, and boots with the white stuff then plead ignorance when she confronted him of "creaming" her. The Nocks could have won an Academy Award for best actor with his denials. Creaming one of us was his just vengeance, the price we paid for being a Larry Cadodee.

Next up on Nock's list for the Halloween pranking who got "creamed" was one of the main ringleaders of the mischief-makers, Darby Donahue. Darby was another popular and beautiful Catholic girl. Her folks owned, operated, and named after themselves the B and I Tavern in downtown Carson City.

Bert and Irene Donahue raised up two daughters destined to become teachers and a son David. Dave was one of Father O'Brien's favorite altar boys who grew up to become a priest. They were all very earthy, sharp-witted people with a great sense of humor.

Darby was a tall and slender with beautiful long curly chestnut hair. She was a pretty girl; her face narrow with sharp features. She was, like her bartender mother, a quick wit and ready to regale the group with a stinging remark. Darby had a hot flash temper too. She clawed to pieces any unfortunate person who triggered her temper in a disagreement.

Darby was a fun friend 99% of the time. She was a queen of cliques, a magnet for all the popular people in school. When she laughed, she had a disarming giggle. It was misleading, making her sound like she was an airhead. But Darby was anything but dumb. She was a top student and the captain of the debate team who won, hands down, every debate she joined.

Like her brother, she was a person of great faith. On religious subjects, she was as pure thinking as Socrates. We imagined Darby might give it all up and become a nun. She admitted she'd considered a nun's life as her future. If she had joined the Convent, it wouldn't have surprised anyone.

Unlike the rest of the group, she didn't quite catch the inner circle of trust because she had an acerbic wit she rarely filtered. Her best friend one day might hold her at arm's length the very next day because of some disparaging remark she'd make. True as it would always be, Darby's remarks were for anyone in hearing range.

She ate lunch at school, but always had a brown bag packed from home. A few days after Halloween she sat down for lunch in the school cafetorium with the cluster of her usual audience of friends including the Nocks. When she opened her bag, it was full of Nock's creamy white revenge. With everyone chuckling, Nocks announced "Looks like some Larry Cadodee found your lunch bag Darby." Darby smiled and nodded her head in agreement, she was a good sport. "Can I borrow your napkins?" she asked everyone in the group as she began cleaning the shaving cream off her lunch.

Because he was home on Halloween, Nocks spared creaming Mark. Monoly was the center of the Catholic group of friends. Or as Nocks might say, he was the head Larry Cadodee.

Mark was a tall and handsome kid with black hair. He was the most popular boy in school. Monoly had an easy laugh and loved to poke fun at everyone, but he would laugh harder when the jokes came back on him. He had his moments of leadership and anyone he asked would join his cause. But most times he was lazy at leadership roles. He preferred to lead only when no one else would. Mark was everyone's friend and moved into any social group of his choosing. But he kept closest to the trusted Catholic school friends Brenna, Darby, and most of all, The Nocks. He played football, basketball, baseball, and ran track, starring in all.

Mark Monolys main purpose in life was to compete in sports. He was always urging teammates on to the ways of winning, hopeless as it seemed in this town of athletic nobodies. Competing to win in sports was his every day goal. He didn't have many other interests other than sports and service to the Church.

Mark was a mainstay in the Monday night CCD classes. He never missed a meeting. The first night in the fall of his senior year was the night when Sister Ann, one of the two nuns left in St. Mary's, became the teacher of the CCD class for the twelfth graders.

The small group of 15 met at the creaky old wood framed convent. There Sister asked them to pull their brown metal folding chairs into an intimate circle for a "rap" session. "Welcome to CCD. Here we will start a long journey into the discovery of your values and the values of Christ as seen through the Church," she said with a warm smile to all of us. "We have simple rules. First, everything is open to discussion. Second, we must always respect each other's opinions. Third, and you'll be glad for this: no homework or tests." This news brought a smile to everyone's face.

She continued, "Tonight I'd like to discuss one of the great challenges the Church has in the world today, protecting the unborn. As you've learned at St. Mary's, the Holy Father has stated that birth control and abortion are sins against the will of God."

Darby was a fervent Catholic, but her Faith didn't stop her from being the early and leading feminist voice in our small group. With red-hot blazing guns, she stepped into the discussion. "Sister," she asked, "what right does the pope have to tell women they can't use birth control pills? For example, what if a married woman is poor and can't afford to get proper medical care and feed a child? What if a poor married woman who already has children and having yet another baby would cause any of her children to suffer from a poverty caused starvation? The point I'm making is this. What if a mother understood she was having another baby and it made it more children than she could support? This baby would cause either the baby to suffer or a new baby would be a threat to her existing children by creating starvation conditions for them. Under these conditions, isn't creating a child be a sin? It would doom this baby and the other children. This would cause a baby or children to starve to death. To give birth to a child you know will kill others, is this not a mortal sin? Is not making a child starve to death the very worst of sins?"

Darby's rapid-fire questions and strong challenge to the teachings of the Church caught Sister Ann off guard. Her look of strong moral leadership that her habit and robes gave her disappeared as Darby overpowered her. Poor Sister looked like a deer caught in the headlights. Nuns and Catholic clergy weren't used to being challenged, especially by high school kids.

She tried to respond. "Now Darby," she started in a firm voice, trying to assert her authority. "No one except God can predict the future" and before she said another word Darby, with her remarkable ability to cut to the quick, interrupted the startled nun.

"Sister, what if I tied you up in a chair and then poured gasoline all over you? Then if I took out a match and struck it, you'd know quick what the future would bring. So, let's not play silly word games. There are times one knows the future in absolute terms. So, would not the larger question be, "Is there a moral obligation to prevent suffering in certain cases, say like rape, birth defects, or extreme poverty? I ask you, is it not the Church's position that to stand by and do nothing to prevent innocents from suffering is a pre-defined and premeditated sin?"

"Now Darby," the nun began. But Darby interrupted. "Sister, the problem is clear. There's a small group of old men who've been running the Church for centuries. They're studying text written by other old men from hundreds and hundreds of years ago. We now have technologies and medicine these men who wrote the Bible never imagined. These elderly men, studying ancient books, they aren't making compassionate choices. We can and we should reduce suffering and sin by using these great medical advances God has given us. Birth control pills can prevent suffering on a massive scale in places in the world where starvation is a daily threat. The Church needs to let women make their own choice about their bodies. Instead, these old men just want to keep women in their subservient place as second-class citizens."

Mark tried his best to rescue the nun by asking Darby, "But Darby, is not the blind use of technology also the way to blind morality? Look at what we're doing in Vietnam with all the weapons we've developed. You can't say using napalm in Vietnam is a virtue? It is a technology used without scruples, a sin against God is it not?" Sister Ann picked up the gauntlet adding "Yes Darby, you see how sinful technology can be without the Lord's guiding hand."

Darby shot back in a calm but firm voice "You're saying the Vietnam War is sinful. But I don't hear Father O'Brien ever talking about it in the pulpit. I don't hear the Pope condemning this war. Sister, I don't hear you saying the war is a sin.

Instead, you preach how women should submit their bodies to the will of the Church, but not one word about Vietnam. Where does the Catholic Church stand on the Vietnam War? I'll tell you Sister; the Church is quiet and supportive. If Jesus was here today, He'd want to end the suffering. He'd want to end the war. He wouldn't be a pilot in Vietnam dropping Napalm, nor would He be silent. It's clear from studying His life that Jesus wouldn't be supporting a bunch of old religious leaders. I'll remind you what you've taught us about Jesus. You've taught us it was old religious leaders who killed Him when He spoke up for peace, love, and compassion."

"Sister, I believe the Church's silence is the coward's choice. The Church uses the pulpit to preach against birth control, to preach against abortion, while it ignores the war in Vietnam. The Church is OK with war but not OK with women making their own choices. I'm convinced the Church persecutes a historical bias against women and would rather go after women than take on the moral implications of a very unjust war. This is a simple case of the Church's moral compass lacking the courage to practice what it preaches."

Sister Ann looked stunned. The first meeting of the 1968 CCD classes sunk into an uncomfortable quiet. In a spontaneous matchup of wits, Darby showed she was the smarter of the two.

The Nocks was at his best when there was an awkward situation and he spoke to end the discomfort in the room. His charms irresistible, he took over the conversation and sent it in a new direction. "Sister," he asked with his most sincere and polite voice. "I wonder if Jesus were alive today and was at a wedding. Let's say some partygoers there were and instead of drinking wine, they were smoking marijuana. If the marijuana ran out, I wonder what Jesus would do? Would He go all modern and turn some weeds into weed?"

Everyone, including Sister Ann, started laughing. The Nocks put a quick end to the tension with his funny question. "Now Richard," Sister answered playfully, she was eager to move on to a lighter subject. "It is my belief Jesus would suggest to the hippies that they should try some of His wine instead. Wine at a wedding is a tradition, you can't have a proper reception without it."

Nocks couldn't hide his smile. He continued on with his tension breaking preposterous question. "I think Jesus would have smoked the dope Sister. He'd agree smoking dope is the smart way to go, no harmful side effects, no liver damage, no hangover, no addiction. I've read in magazines if we all had a choice to make in a neutral environment, we'd all choose the weed over alcohol. It's healthier, natural, there's no danger to it."

Shy Brenna chimed in, "You can't fool me Nocks, you and your Larry Cadodee pals would do both at the wedding." This lit the Nocks up, he started laughing out loud at the surprising utterance from the timid member of the group.

When Nock's laughing ebbed a bit, Sister Ann asked a serious question. "Have any of you used marijuana or drugs?" She asked meekly as she looked around the circle, looking each person in the eye. Nocks replied as only he could. "None of us have Sister, how about you, you're the one here living in a commune like the hippies, have you got something to confess to the group?" Everyone started laughing again at the absurd thought of Sister Ann smoking dope.

"No, Richard," she said, smiling and holding back her own laughter. "I see why people think we Dominicans might be hippies. We all have love beads, we carry them everywhere," and she grinned and held up the rosary she carried on her waist. The Nocks continued his unsuccessful deadpan, "I'm not sure about you Sister, you're always so pleasant, smiling, wearing boots, same clothes every day, you live in a commune. I say you're a hippie!" Darby, realizing Nocks was defusing the tension she'd created, joined in the lighthearted teasing. "Sister, are you sure you're not smoking something?" and Sister replied, "Darby, I'm high on Jesus" and Nocks started laughing all over again saying "There's got to be a bong in this convent somewhere."

My sister says drugs are everywhere at her college," Brenna whispered when the laughter died down. The group's full attention now came to her. "Dad says it's almost like a new disease is breaking out. With drugs and everything else going on, my heart breaks when I see where our society is heading.

Every night on television, I see videos from Vietnam. Soldiers are shooting guns and cannons. Refugees are fleeing for their lives. They evacuate the wounded on helicopters. There always seems to be rows of dead Vietnamese lined up for "body counts." "It scares me," she mumbled, her voice shaking. "I just can't understand why anyone can be so cruel."

Brenna's large brown eyes peeked out from under her dark bangs as she looked for comfort from her friends and the nun all gathered together in the circle. Her frightening view of the world sobered the small group of friends. She wasn't the great student like almost everyone else in the group. Brenna was insecure by nature, but when she voiced her distress, the most innocent and helpless lamb in our little herd crying out for help touched all of us.

Darby reached over and put her hand on Brenna's

shoulder to reassure her by saying, "I feel the same way sometimes." She looked first at Brenna and then to everyone else. "Do you remember when we were in the 4th grade in Catholic School and we practiced the duck and roll under our desks in case there was a nuclear bomb? I've had many nightmares from it. I can't understand why anyone would aim a missile at our school to burn us all. How horrible it would be to burn. Now I look back and wonder what nut recommends hiding under a school desk to save us from an atomic bomb blast."

"I wondered if we were lucky to survive a bomb blast, wouldn't we just end up starving to death in the Church Hall?" Darby said. "The Black and Orange Civil Defense signs are still on the walls at the entrance to the Hall. I guess it's still the place where we're still supposed to run for shelter if we're attacked. But if we tried to hide there and stay for days after a nuclear attack, what are we supposed to eat? It's a shelter with no food. I think how awful it would be in the basement of the Hall with a nuclear war and fallout all around us. The radiation outside would just keep us stuck in a cellar. We'd all just be sitting there in the basement hungry. We'd all starve to death. It's so stupid. It's not a rational plan."

Mark, like everyone in the now somber group, had been listening and was now careful with his words before he spoke, "I feel the same way Darby. I remember when I was about 10 years old going outside with my dad one October night and sitting out on the back porch in the cold air. We'd just listened to President Kennedy on TV during the Cuban Missile Crisis. Our fear was the Communists in Cuba could nuke us in just a few minutes. I can remember sitting there with my dad and his having his arm around me as we looked up in the sky to see if any missiles were coming. Dad said not to worry as we shivered in the cold surveilling the night sky, watching for incoming missiles. I can't tell you how afraid I was. I was certain that an atomic bomb was on its way to kill us." Mark said, "I've read a bit about the Russians and what their plan is and it is scary. With Lansing just 40 miles away, I'm sure the Russians will have that city targeted to wipe out the automobile factories. From what I learned about Soviet Missile technology; they can't hit much more than about 20 miles from what they're targeting. To compensate for their lack of accuracy, they put bigger bombs on their missiles. If they don't kill us directly with an atomic bomb, we wouldn't live long enough to starve to death. We'll be glowing like light bulbs from the radiation."

"Thanks for the happy thoughts Mark," Nocks said as he tried again to break the tension in the room with a little sarcasm, "You've made us all feel better."

"I love you guys, but it's not funny," said Brenna. "I just wonder what's wrong with us. We're killing people in Vietnam, we've killed President Kennedy, we killed Bobby Kennedy, and we killed Martin Luther King. Anyone who speaks up and wants peace and love, we kill them. I pray we just stop this killing and

71

we just all live a happy life. It's what I want. I want a happy life. I don't want to live in fear anymore."

Sister Ann leaned forward in her chair to communicate to us she was listening and concerned for each member of the group. When the evening was ending, she took over the discussion and tried to give a reassuring summary. "We live in a world we question, a world full of evil and fear," she began. "It's been this way through history. Jesus came to show us the light, for truth and justice, and if you follow Him you will find refuge in any storm. Tonight, I ask you to join hands for a few minutes and say a Hail Mary for peace." Sister stood up and held her hands out, and everyone rose to their feet and joined her in a circle, everyone holding each other's hands.

The group all said the prayer together, "Hail Mary Full of Grace the Lord is with thee. Blessed art thou among women and blessed is the fruit of thy womb, Jesus. Holy Mary Mother of God pray for us sinners now and at the hour of our death. Amen."

After they recited the prayer, Sister said, "Peace be with each of you." Yet Brenna was still in distress. Her eyes were misty. She had spoken with touching vulnerably to the fears all us felt as we grew up in the 1960s. The sins of the world found us despite living as we did, in relative seclusion in this little farm town in the middle of Michigan.

Mark saw Brenna was close to tears, so he came up to her and put his arms around her. He pulled her tenderly into his chest and gave her a protective hug. "Don't worry Brenna, I'll watch out for you," he said as he held her with his chin resting on the top of her head.

Brenna and Mark had a long history. They played together in preschool, had first communion and confirmation together, and attended grade school together. Brenna and Mark traded comic books in Catholic junior high and headed over to the public school together. They shared those bonds with everyone at CCD. She had spoken from her heart and touched Mark and the group. She nestled her head into his chest further, as if hiding away from the troubled world. One by one, everyone but the nun surrounded them and leaned in to put their head to her shoulder, or place an affectionate hand to her head. Brenna was the most innocent and tender person in the group, everyone wanted to comfort and protect her."

# Chapter 3 *Communications*

"Your Mother is texting me and asking what time we'll be getting home", I report to Molly who's happily driving the Jeep along what has now become a cloudless sunny spring day in West Michigan, "I'll let her know we will get back to the house a little after dusk." I add. Molly nods her head to acknowledge she's heard me, pauses as she catches a thought, then asks "As a kid growing up Dad, did your parents make you text them while you ran around the hayfields with your buddies?"

Her question, especially the jab, gives me a quiet chuckle. I appreciate that she is coming to maturity in the age of instant communications. She doesn't remember only a few years ago, when our family had a landline before the age of cell phones. "Uh no," I say, "Cell phones hadn't made it to the drawing board back in the 1960s. My favourite TV show was the first version of "Star Trek." The crew on the spaceship each having a personal telecommunicator intrigued me. I dreamed of a portable telephone but never thought they would be a reality in my lifetime. To me, it is amazing everyone has a smart phone with instant communications to almost everywhere in the world.

I don't think your generation appreciates the marvel of instant worldwide communications. To you it's routine and normal. Your generation doesn't consider what a miracle you have in the palm of your hands. The magic escapes your notice. In the rare instances when a call drops, you'll complain, "I've only got one bar here, Verizon sucks!"

In my lifetime, technology has changed the way we communicate. The world I grew up in was larger. When I was growing up communicating from a distance had its complexities. The limitations contributed to making our exchanges more meaningful and thoughtful.

For example, a "long distance" phone call in its self would be a special event. For the average family, a long-distance phone call happened for very special occasions, such as an engagement announcement or a death in the family. Because of the expense, we couldn't be frivolous with this kind of communication. Quite a contrast to today where Molly, you think nothing of sending pictures of your morning stack of pancakes to your pals without a thought as to where they                        might                        be.

When I was 10 years old, my sister attended college 40 miles away from home in Lansing. The family would get excited to hear from her when she made a rare long-distance telephone call. Unlike now, "long-distance" phone calls cost a lot of money, charges added up by the minute. To make matters worse, the connections were often unreliable and unclear. The expense of the calls made them an infrequent but special family event.

During one of her calls to home, everybody in the

family would take a turn on the phone. Dad hovered nearby tapping his wristwatch to let you know your time on his phone took money out of his wallet. We'd hurriedly be talking about whatever hot topic we held dear until Dad would put an end to your conversation by announcing "Times up." He'd queue up the next family member for their chance to talk. These calls became some of the best family memories, everyone delighting in the modern marvel of being able to talk to far away loved ones.

Sometimes a call came "person to person", which meant that the caller had requested an operator dial the requested phone number and ask for a specific person to receive it. The operator would ask for the desired person to take the call. If the specified person didn't identify themselves, no charges went to the bill. My folks, like a lot of families would, on rare occasions when a family member would be out of town for a night, required the traveller to call home "person to person" and inquire for themselves. Whoever answered the call would answer truthfully that the recipient couldn't pick up the call. "Person to person" calls like these let the traveller tell the homebodies they'd arrived at their destination and, above all else next to being safe, avoid all telephone charges. My folks and most of their friends grew up poor in the Great Depression. Wanting to save a few dollars came from the values they developed as penniless kids.

Carson City's phone company installed a brand-new phone system in 1965. That ended the switch board system and started a new era of rotary dials and dial tones.  In the old system, the caller picked up the receiver, and a locally employed switchboard operator, always a woman, asked the caller for the number to call.  Then she then plugged wires into the switchboard to connect the caller to the person called.

The new self-dial system allowed for folks to pay a premium and have a private line, but most families in Carson City didn't have a lot of extra money for such luxuries.  Instead, almost everyone shared a phone line, called a party line, with 4 or 5 other homes. When anyone from those party line families used the telephone, no one else could make or receive a call. Anyone with a "party line" could also hear and speak to anyone on the "party line" when anyone in the "party" was talking on the telephone.  That meant party lines were very susceptible to eavesdroppers.

Small towns had a particular etiquette for party lines. For example, polite people would cut short their phone conversations if someone on the shared line picked up their phone to make a call.  But some people were not considerate of their party liners.  The worst offenders talking for a long time on the party lines were lovesick teenagers.  People trying to make a call when a "line hog" was yakking sometimes abandoned politeness and started clicking the button repeatedly on the receiver-rest to anonymously annoy those whose conversations took up too much time.

But most party liners tried to be polite phone neighbours.   It was acceptable to interrupt the conservants to inquire how long the line would be "tied up." Although it was a breach of etiquette to eavesdrop on a conversation, it happened. Mischievous kids, and more adults than would admit, secretly listened in on other's conversations.

The late 1960s were the last throes of the telegraph age. Carson City's Western Union Telegraph service had been operating since the early 1870s beginning when the railroad came to town. It was a special event to get an occasional telegraph. There were times when Mark had a great basketball or football game when he got a phone call from the Western Union office at the Central Bean and Grain elevators. They'd call to inform him he'd received a telegraph.

It was a short walk to the dusty old Central Bean and Grain office at the north edge of town. There he'd pick up a message inside a Western Union yellow envelope. It would be from his grandparents when they were wintering in Florida, wiring to congratulate him on a game well played. They would read about one of Mark's high school team's exploits in the Carson City Gazette, which they received through the mail. If the team won or Mark's name got mentioned in the article, his grandparents wired their congratulations. They had used the old technology their entire lives. Their comfort level with this old system was high, and it was cheaper than a long-distance phone call. Over time, Mark grew to enjoy the telegraphs and shared them with his closest friends.

Mark enthusiastically opened those bright yellow envelopes right there in the old dusty Western Union office at Central Bean and Grain. He'd read the message amid the smells from wheat, oats, soybeans, and corn in the air. He'd read the notes while the old telegraph clicked its peculiar rhythms in the background. What helped make a telegraph message so interesting to read was that the sender would use as few words as possible, almost like a twitter feed, to keep the Western Union per word charges as low as possible. Also, instead of a period, sentences in a telegraph ended with the word "STOP."

Mark's Grandpa would always have a clever way to include the STOP at the end of a sentence, like "Having fun playing football don't STOP. Or "Hear you're dating the Smith girl she's cute don't STOP. "If she's a good kisser, don't STOP." "I hear she's asking you for money so tell her STOP."

One typical winter's night at the Monoly dinner table the diminutive Mrs. Monoly announced that she had received a letter from Mark's Grandparents who were staying the season in sunny Florida. I've saved it for dessert." she announced, and with that Mark groaned and said "Geeze Mom, I have stuff to do after dinner, can't I read it later?" "Young man, let's not go against Momma's wishes", Mom Monoly playfully shot back. Mark was up for the challenge "Who's stopping me if I get up and leave Mrs. Short Stuff"? Mrs. Monoly replied with her typical humour, putting her hands on her hips to accentuate the comical confrontation, "Better watch out mister, you might be bigger than me but don't you forget that dynamite comes in small packages!" and both Mrs. Monoly and Mark got a good laugh. When the moment passed, she picked up the subject once again, "Seriously," she continued on, "it's a special treat to get a letter from someone, it should make your day."

She explained, "It's special when a friend or relative takes the time to write a letter, so our reading it as a family event is a compliment to the writer. I enjoy reading a personal letter at the end of a dinner, like a desert." She opened the letter and handed it to Mark. "You go first," she said. "Read it and pass it to your sister." Mark did a quick read and handed it to his sister, who took a few minutes more to read the correspondence. She passed it to his dad, who gave it a careful reading and then at last, he passed it to Mark's mother.

Mark's mother put on a pair of her cat eyed reading glasses and read it with care. She finished and handed it back to Mark. Switching her tone of voice from playful to an encouraging and teaching tone of voice she prodded, "Read it again Mark, inspect it this time." Mark took the letter again and looked at it while she continued. "You see it's handwritten, like all the best letters. Grandma's handwriting is so beautiful." Mark nodded in agreement as he examined the letter with increasing interest in the details. He agreed, the penmanship was exquisite.

"The penmanship and writing style of the writer is as interesting as the content of the letter.", she explained. "Look at the great care Grandma has taken; she's writing with an old-style fountain pen. She's drawing ink right out of an inkwell; you can tell by the purple tint you see in the lighter strokes. It's hard to do. She wrote it and didn't drop a single blot of ink on the letter. She took extraordinary care writing each word. Few folks have the skills to use an old-style fountain pen. It's becoming a lost art. A novice with a fountain pen would have drip marks and inkblots everywhere. Penning this document was an endeavour. It's humbling to realize another person thinks you are deserving of so much effort and care." Mark, now engaged in the letter's analysis, looked up from the letter and said "Wow Mom, you're right, I've never given it much thought. I can see how much effort Grandma put into her letters to us.

A hand-written letter is a craft, a way to communicate the high esteem in which the author holds the reader. When Grandma scripted this letter, the care and exactness took time and effort, and as our eyes follow the stroke of every J or H, the care she's taking makes me feel good because of the flair she's displaying. I get letters from friends sometimes and it can be just the opposite if they've just "sent a hasty note." In those cases, I feel like I'm not of much importance to them.

"You're right Mom," Mark said, "I'm seeing a lot more in this letter now that I examine it. It's a wonderful letter, and she's written on her special stationery with no lines, and the script is true. Her margins line up as straight as the paper's edges. I don't know how she does it. How can she get the spacing so exact?"

"I can tell you this, we're not reading the first draft of this letter", Mrs. Monoly answered, I have a special place for this letter because it is so well composed in every sense of the word, it's an important document and artful enough to put into the family scrapbook. We'll keep it right along with our treasured photographs. It's so well done I'll keep it is a permanent memento of Grandma. We'll enjoy reading this letter again years from now. It will be something we'll treasure long after she's gone."

In the den of the modest Monoly home was the family writer's desk. They used it exclusively for composing personal letters. The side drawer held a well-thumbed thesaurus. Next to it the family dictionary. Anyone who needed a quiet place found the desk a good place to write, the family heirloom fountain pen and stationery, all there patiently waiting for a writer.

Mark wrote back in kind to his grandparents. He went to work at the desk, writing a plain draft in pencil on a lined piece of paper. He edited it with the help of his mom, then re-wrote it on stationery with the best penmanship he could muster. He knew the reading process on the receiving end was just like the one at home and he wanted his Grandparents to know he was trying his level best to equal their efforts. Back then we didn't use the word "love" much. Instead, one could show love through a well scripted and thoughtful letter. There in the letter, for all to see, tangible evidence of our affections.

The Monoly family would receive letters from Uncle Rene and Aunt Mary in Clearwater, Florida, or someone on vacation in New York City. In every case, the letters became the central topic of conversation at family dinners. They scrutinized the stamp and the postmark. Was the letter airmailed? What kind of stamp? The postmark told the time in delivery. Someone would always say, "It's hard to believe just a few days ago this very piece of paper", was in San Francisco, Tampa, or from wherever it originated. We examined every bit of information from these letters like detectives. The family discussed their findings with delight. Reading these hand written letters, just as Mom Monoly said, were like a dessert.

Sometimes the news was bad. Such a letter might spread through our tiny town in a hot flash, going through our homes in a heartbeat. On one of those occasions, we learned Mike Collins, one of the last graduates of St. Mary's high school, had a near death experience.

Mike was a typical kid from Carson City. After graduating from high school he'd taken a job in nearby Alma working as a Ma Bell lineman. A few months later, he became the first man from Carson in the Vietnam Era to be an Army draftee. When he went into the service, the town was interested in his well-being regardless of their support or lack thereof for the war. Being drafted is big news in a small-town and the word travels at light speed, it burns through the merchants, over the phones, moving person to person everywhere. The news never travelled faster on this network than when Mike Collins wrote his parents to tell them he was soon heading to the airport and from there flying out to his assignment, Vietnam.

The shocker came the very next day. A long-distance phone call from the Pentagon notified Mike's parents that Mike got wounded in Vietnam. The medial staff in Vietnam evacuated him to a US Army hospital in Japan.

Later Mike said he had served the shortest tour in Vietnam of any other soldier. He'd arrived at his camp in Vietnam and before he could even unpack his bags, received orders to go on patrol. Just a few "clicks" outside the camp, Mike took a sniper's bullet in his shoulder. Front line medics evacuated him on a medical helicopter, the start of his transport to a US Army hospital in Japan. It all happened during his single day in Vietnam."

Our Jeep hit a hard bump. It jolted us for a second. "Vietnam was always overshadowing everything for us Molly. Almost every night on the evening news it was the lead story, and we had only three channels on our TV so watching the evening news was a daily event. But as a kid growing up, TV lacked the feel of reality. The wounding of Mike Collins hit us kids like a lightning bolt. It shot us in our hearts. Having one of our own become a war causality hardened those of us who were against the war and softened forever those who supported it. The adults in our town took it the same way."

"Did he recover?" asked Molly. "It sounds like a movie, being shot in the shoulder, you know, a flesh wound." "Movies never cover the aftermath" I reply, "Mike spent months in therapy, had multiple surgeries, and had chronic pain the rest of his life. He earned a degree on the G.I. bill and worked at nearby Central Michigan University as a counsellor. But the constant pain in his shoulder never went away and most of us believe his early death 20 years later was because of his seeking pain relief by taking pain pills. It didn't help that his post Army life became daily indulgences with heavy drinking."

This information genuinely touched Molly, "So sad" she said. "Sure is." I said. "Mike had many friends and came from a respected family. The sadness doesn't stop with him either, there are many more just like him. Vietnam was such a huge waste. We were used to seeing Vietnam on TV every day, maybe that made us calloused or maybe it made the war seem surreal, but the war became more real the day Mike Collins got shot."

## Chapter 4 *Harvest Time*

Miss Molly can't go long without food or a little snack. She is a thin little gal, which belies her voracious appetite and large food capacity. It's no surprise when she slows the Jeep down at the outskirts of the crossroads town of Fruitport and gives me her little devious grin and says, "Slurpee?"

There is nothing she loves more than to introduce one of her favorite treats to someone, and she's shown me the delights of 7 Eleven's signature refreshment. She pulls hard on the steering wheel and we fly into the 7 Eleven parking lot with a bump and a jarring stop before I can say a word. As my head recoils backwards from her slamming hard on the brakes, I say with a grin, "I guess it just wouldn't be right to drive right by a Pina Colada Slurpee and not get one."

We Slurpee up at the drinks fountain. It's a neat little store and we're the only two customers. Molly fills her mega 32-ounce cup first and heads up the aisle to the cashier ahead of me. She playfully announces, with a flip of the thumb at me several steps behind, that "The old dude is buying today." The store clerk's bewildered look makes me realize that she hasn't yet put Molly and I together as a father-daughter act.

The store clerk's reaction makes me remember what is never in the front my mind. We adopted Molly when she was a baby. Molly's not Irish like me but a full-blooded Korean, something our family and friends, blinded by the love we have for her, just keep forgetting. The poor lady's face changes quickly from puzzlement to enlightenment as I come up to the counter. With a sideways nod of the head in Molly's direction, I say to the now bemused lady that "I'll pay because this old dude has a job and so as a result, I have my money to spend, unlike some freeloader I know, not to point fingers at anyone." Standing at the door impatiently, Molly rolls her eyes as she puckers up her face with the first slurp of her slurpee.

The clerk's eyes light up as I've confirmed that yes, we are a father and a daughter, and she quickly buys into the game. She teases Molly with a warm maternal voice, "Honey, I'm sure you've heard every one of your Dad's "when I was a boy, I had to work stories." Grinning wide and giving another Hollywood eye roll, Molly says, "Yes, I have. Millions of them," and she opens the door of the store, waiting for me to pay. After my credit card zips through, I stage whisper to the Molly as we head out the door in earshot of the smiling clerk, "I've got lots or stories you haven't heard yet!"

I call out "Shotgun!" as I slide into the passenger's seat as Molly rolls over the Jeep's engine. I continue my recollections of the jobs I worked as a youth. "Would you like to hear how we used to bale hay back in the day?" I buckle my seat belt and take a sip of my delicious Pina Colada. "Nooooo" says Molly dramatically. "Yesssss" I reply, matching her intensity. We share a merry laugh as she pulls the Jeep out of the parking lot and back on the road. I tease her with "You'll love hearing what it was like baling hay, there was lots of good food involved."

This results in another teenager's eye-roll and I go for it. I tell Molly that "For a dollar an hour, very good pay for any farm town kid, we boys could bale hay for about 6 weeks every summer, maybe eight weeks if there was a "fourth cut." One more than the normal three, the extra cut meant a perfect farming summer was coming. Farmers considered a fourth cut was Mother Nature's bonus crop and a sign of a coming prosperous year on the farm. The extra harvest gave the farmers and the hay baling crews a much-appreciated opportunity to make a few more dollars.

Work found us Catholic boys; we didn't need to make a call to farmers to ask to bale hay. Instead, we'd get a pull on the elbow as we were leaving Sunday Mass from a farmer or his wife inquiring if we were free to come harvest the hay. Through the Church, they knew us well. The farmers preferred altar boys. They believed serving Mass made us punctual and reliable. They socialized with our families and knew whose folks had zero tolerance for laziness. Our parents made sure we got the State required work permit that certified for the farmers we were at least 14 years old.

For us teenagers, the best thing about baling hay, besides the big money, was there were no early morning hours. After the farmers mowed hay, it had to dry. They drove the tractors that mowed or pulled the special rake that ran the hay cuttings into little straight lines of hay. The field work started at daybreak. Before the last step of baling, rolling of lines of sweet-smelling fresh cut hay continued over and over until the sun dried out all the moisture.

A bale was about 4 ft. long, 2 ft. square and weighed about 70 lbs. If bales were heavier, it meant the hay had a high moisture content. We couldn't bale wet hay because it produced dangerous methane gas. Methane gas in a barn would set a barn on fire or, worse yet, blow it to pieces from a spark off a light switch. Farmers used the morning sun to dry the dew off the hay before baling could start each day. When the sun rose in the sky it dried the hay and with raking, it normally was ready for bailing at noon. That meant we boys could sleep in late in our teenage slumber before heading to the farms for a day's work.

A day in the hay mound on a Michigan June, July, or August day was sweltering hot, dirty, hard work. The hay mound in the barn would be hotter than a sidewalk on the Fourth of July and dusty, the air full of hay chaff from hay bales. Rough brown binder twine held the bales together. Without gloves, our tender city-boy hands wouldn't make it through a day. A light long-sleeved shirt was a must, especially if you were allergic to hay, to keep the hay from scratching up forearms. The long sleeves were a good tradeoff. Better comfort for being a little hotter.

Our favorite farm to bale hay was Mark's aunt and uncle, Alice and Kyran O'Conner. Respected in the community as successful farmers, Kyran and Alice owned an 80-acre "Centennial Farm," a Michigan designation for farms owned by the same family for a minimum of 100 years. Kyran was 60 years old, 6 ft. tall and barrel chested. He was fit and trim, weighed around 200 pounds and had pure white hair and a friendly smile. His hair and smile both glowed in the sunshine.

Kyran was a straight-talking, devout Catholic who'd raised four wonderful kids with his schoolteacher wife. They were the hardest working farmers we knew, seldom seen much around town in the summer. The exception being Sunday Mass. In winter, they had leisure time and spent much of it socializing. The O'Conners were pillars of the Church, he always in attendance in his blue suit, white shirt, and fashionable necktie on Sundays, the norm for most men attending Church in those days.

For Church Alice wore a nice skirt, a proper modest blouse, and a scarf to cover her jet-black hair she kept in a tight bun. She looked every bit the schoolmarm she was. She was tall, thin, and had a stern look about her that misrepresented her glorious sense of humor and love of fun.

Kyran and Alice O'Conner were proud Irish Catholics. They had pleasant dispositions and affable smiles. They were fun to be with. They had an aura of goodness about them. Everyone in Carson, Catholic and non-Catholic, knew the O'Conners and loved them for their good humor and countless acts of kindness.

Years earlier, during the Great Depression, Mark's paternal grandparents and their family lived with the O'Conners on the farm. This cohabitation came after Grandpa Monoly lost his business. The economic disaster claimed the Monoly's home, and eventually Grandpa Monoly's health. Mark's grandparents, like many families in the Great Depression, were desperate and destitute. Kyran and Alice came to their rescue. They invited them to come "help" with the farm, sparring the Monoly's the cruel fate at the hands of bankers. The O'Conners insisted on sharing their 5-bedroom, two story farm home with the Monolys. It was on there on the O'Conners farm Mark's dad spent his formative years as his family struggled back to their feet.

As a kid growing up, Mark teased the O'Conner's that someday, if he encountered something catastrophic, he would follow the family tradition and come live with them on the farm. He would say to Aunt Alice, "If a day comes when I lose everything I have in the world, Aunt Alice, I believe I could come to the farm and you'd take me and my family in." She'd laugh and rear her head back, then give him a serious look straight in the eye and reply, "Yes you could," and then after a slight pause she'd announce in her strict schoolmarm voice, "But there will be work." There was no doubt she meant it. When working in the fields, Kyran wore his faded green overalls with the matching green cap for protection from the sun. Hay baling was almost always during the sunniest of days.

Kyran always ran the baler. We kids drove a lot of the farm equipment but none of us ever ran the baler. It was expensive and a complicated piece of equipment. It needed a lot of in the field maintenance and could be dangerous to fix. Kyran didn't want us to get hurt and we appreciated his concern for our well-being.

The hay baling operation included a portable elevator placed outside the barn, stretching from the ground to the peak of the roof. It looked kind of like a big long sled with a chain loop going up. It had metal slates that would catch a bale of hay and slide it up to the top of the elevator. An older tractor made runs between the field and the barn, pulling wagon load after wagon load of hay up to the elevator. Coming from the hayfields, the tractor would pull up to the side of the barn with the wagon bulging full of fresh cut sweet smelling hay. Then the manual process of unloading the hay wagons would begin.

The elevator ran off the power take-off on the old green John Deere tractor, a spinning shaft on the end of the tractor that connected to the elevator to power it. There were a few minutes spent hooking it up before we would start running the grids up to the barn. An excellent team of guys would shift around the responsibilities, sometimes running the wagon, other times working up in the mow. The mow was the worst because of the heat and the hay chaff, the green, dusty floating debris caused by the hay bales dropping from the elevator, so it was great not to be in the mow all day long.

In the middle of the afternoon during a 2nd cut harvest, it was Mark's turn to drive the old John Deere tractor and empty hay wagon down the dusty lane to the hayfields where Kyran was running the baler. Before departing Mark stopped at the house to bring along a thermos full of ice-cold, freshly squeezed lemonade. Kyran would be hot and thirsty, and Aunt Alice made it special just for him.

As he pulled the tractor onto the field and drove up alongside Kyran, Mark waved the stainless-steel thermos up in the air for Kyran to see, bringing an instant bright smile from underneath the old green cap. They both turned off the noisy tractors and climbed down from the driver's seats, "Mark," Kyran said happily "You are a sight to see, what did your Aunt Alice send along with you?" Mark answered "Lemonade, Aunt Alice says you love her lemonade almost as much as you love her." "That's true, but I'd choose her every time," said Kyran, "Grab a bale off the wagon and we'll find a piece of shade alongside the tractor and take a break. Your Aunt Alice knows what a real treat lemonade is in these hay fields in the hot late summer sun." Kyran always appreciated the smallest of things. Mark strived to please him. He was a gentle, kind man we all liked a lot.

Kyran poured the cold lemonade into the built-in cup of the thermos and handed it to Mark saying, "Here you go Mark, you drink from the cup. I'll drink straight from the thermos." He extended the thermos for a little clink and a wink as he gave an Irish toast, "May the good Lord take a liking to you, but not too soon!" Kyran took a big swig from the thermos and wiped his mouth on his green sleeve in complete satisfaction. "Now nephew, may I ask what are you going to do with all the money you're making here on the farm this summer?"

"I might spend a few dollars on some albums and a movie, but most of it goes to my college fund." "Good for you," Kyran replied. "Aunt Alice graduated from Central Teacher's College and never regretted getting her degree. The money she makes as a teacher helped us out during some leaner years we've experienced here on the farm too."

Mark asked, "How did you become a farmer?" Kyran chuckled and shook his head before replying. "Never had a choice, I was born in the farmhouse, lived my entire life in it. This farm is the same place where my dad was born and lived his life. His dad, your maternal great-great-grandfather Denny O'Conner, came here from Ireland. Grandpa Denny left Ireland because he was in grave danger. He left with nothing more than the clothes on his back to escape starvation during in the great Potato Famine in the late 1840s. He made it here, ended up buying this land, and no first-born male O'Conner, and that includes me and my dad, ever left it. Grandpa told me once, when I was a boy, how incredibly ironic it was that the finger of God saved him from famine, put him on this rich farmland, and from this very spot, the old failed Irish potato farmer lived on and fed the masses.

It's quite a story Mark. When I look at the fence lines bordering the fields, I imagine how Denny O'Connor measured these boundaries, put down the fence posts. He sacrificed so much to come here. I think about him leaving everything and everyone he knew in Ireland to come to this place. When I consider all he did, I am forever grateful he passed this farm down to us. It gives me the motivation to continue what he started.

So, as they say, Let's make hay while the sun shines," and Kyran laughed out loud as he pulled himself up from the bale of hay. He extended a hand to Mark and helped him up from their makeshift bench in the middle of Denny O'Connor's field. "I say that every morning to your Aunt Alice during hay season and she rolls her eyes and tells me I'm pushing my luck.

Back at the barn it took a 45-minute turn around until

the next full hay wagon came up from the fields. This gave the mow crew time to climb down to the dairy below and scoop out a gallon of ice-cold whole milk from the morning milking.

State law requires farmers to store their milk in stainless steel vats before shipping it to creameries for processing. The temperature in those vats is much colder than a household refrigerator. The unprocessed milk is a degree or two above freezing. All the while, the vat gently stirs the cold milk. The stirring prevents the raw milk from separating into butter or whatever else unstirred whole milk becomes.

Nothing makes you appreciate how good near freezing milk is than working a sweltering day in a haymow. Kyran and Alice encouraged us to drink all we wanted. One of us would climb up on a stepladder to the small door on top of the stainless-steel vat and scoop out a plastic pitcher full of ice-cold milk from the white swirling mass. The milk was a welcome relief during the breaks between stacking the hay in the dirty, hot, dusty haymow. We'd also fetch pitchers of milk from the vat for dinner.

Nothing's better for a hay baling crew member than dinner time. The farmer's wives knew we boys were ravenous, and we'd come in from the barn ready to eat. All afternoon Aunt Alice, assisted by her daughters and granddaughters, worked in the kitchen baking and cooking. Alice O'Conner was wise. She reasoned that with all the farms paying us boys at the same rate, the limited labor force would choose the farm perceived to be a better place to work. So she served sumptuous meals that became a local legend and gave the O'Connor harvests a huge recruiting edge.

Around 5 pm the whole hay baling operation would stop and about 8 to 12 hungry kids would move out from the barns up to the house for some great home cooking. We'd all wash up, using the garden hose on the side of the house to wash out the grime and sweat off our skin and hair. Most of us boys would have a second shirt to put on so we could be at least half clean for the dinner table.

We'd pitch in and help carry the O'Conner's heavy cherry wood dining room table and chairs outdoors and set up in the cool shade between the side of the house and under the giant maple tree in the yard. There the women would spread out every great tasting fresh food on the farm. Alice insured we had plenty to eat. She waited on us hand and foot.

Aunt Alice would have fried chicken, baked potatoes, fresh salads, homemade bread, fresh baked pies, cakes, cookies, beans, corn on the cob, ham, meatloaf, pasta, jellies, preserves, apples, peaches, and cherries. Almost all the food fresh. Most grown right there on the farm. She'd share with us Kyran's favorite freshly squeezed lemonade and on some days homemade ice cream ground away in a mixer as we boys devoured dinner. She would encourage us

97

to enjoy the meal and eat all we could. Every time we sat at her table, Alice and Kyran never failed to voice appreciation for the hard the work we did during the harvest of hay. She watched us with satisfaction as we ate; she loved seeing us eat. Everybody at the table thanked her profusely during and after the great outdoor meals.

Dinner was always fun. Everyone enjoyed the break in the day from the hot and sweaty labor. The meals provided time for the team to bond and enjoy each other's company. No one was immune from being the target of good-natured teasing, Kyran always in the center of the fun making. His quick-wits and easy laugh made us giggle with delight. He typically would start it out by singling one of us from town out and tease us, calling each one of us "soft pretty city boys."

Every dinner the team divided into two groups, the "dumb farmers" and "soft pretty city boys." Kyran headed up the farm team, he boasted they were farm smart and he took great delight in good-naturedly picking on us town boys. He put our wits to the test. We soft pretty city boys found truth in the old saying that declared, "There are old farmers and there are dumb farmers, but there are no old dumb farmers."

None of us were a match for Kyran O'Conner. He could turn any of us inside out. He'd go around the table to pick on each one of us "soft pretty city boys" by telling the farm boys how he'd pranked each one of us. He'd get everyone howling with laughter as he reminisced, sometimes even telling the truth, about the time that he'd sent out one of us soft pretty city boys out to the pigsty to get the pig milk, or having had us looking under a sleeping rooster for eggs, or setting us up to milk a cow when we had no clue how. The fun part was mostly true when he said we were "soft pretty city boys."

But being "soft pretty city boys" didn't make us defenseless. Every once in a while, he'd get a swift retort to one of his zingers. He'd laugh as hard as the rest of us when a "soft pretty city boy" would ask him, as a representative of dumb farmers everywhere, if he ever heard of toilet paper? One of our favorites was to ask him, "When did he first realize traffic lights weren't Christmas decorations?"

Mark got even with him once by comically telling the work crew, "Uncle Kyran and Aunt Alice O'Conner look so proper coming to church every Sunday. Uncle Kyran in his nice blue suit, Aunt Alice in her best dress, hat, white gloves and matching purse. Hard to believe they could look so crisp and snappy riding to town on their big green John Deere Tractor. They are proud farmers and you know Uncle Kyran, we're all wondering," Mark asked facetiously, "Uncle Kyran, do you come to town on the roads or across the fields?" Before Kyran could respond Mark continued by saying "There's a rumor in town that Uncle Kyran drives across the fields He drives that way because if met with a stop sign on a road, Uncle Kyran and Aunt Alice would obey the sign, stop, and then in frustration, turn around, go back home and never see the inside of a Church."

"Alice!" Kyran called out to include her in the joke, "You know that's not a terrible idea, think of the money we'd save by driving the tractor and using our tax-free farm gas to get to church?" Alice deadpanned, "Now Kyran I just want to be on time for church, if you want to save a dollar or two per year driving the tractor to church, okay. All I ask is that you keep that tractor washed up and keep a good shine on it every Sunday. I don't want to go to church on a dirty tractor." Her response drew hoots of laughter from all of us at the table.

The fun wasn't complete until Kyran told a tall tale or two. His favorite stories contrasted the realities of farm life compared to the naivety of city slickers. One of our favorites was his yarn about Waldo, his 3-legged wonder pig. Kyran said that "a city slicker was driving by and spotted Waldo the 3-legged pig and stopped by to ask him how the pig had lost his leg. "I told him that there was a time when I was working the fields on a tractor when the tractor rolled over and trapped me. The tractor kept running and was spinning wildly. Waldo saw my peril and kicked down the pigpen fence and ran to my aid. He bit down on my collar and pulled me to safety. He saved me from being crushed to death underneath the runaway tractor."

This impressed the city slicker. But he still hadn't got

an answer of how Waldo lost his leg.  So, he inquired about the missing pig's leg again but Kyran said he digressed, "When the kids were young, they were waiting one icy winter morning on the side of the road for the school bus to come.  A car came speeding over the hill and lost control and was heading right at them.  The kids stood there frozen in fear while that out-of-control car came bearing down on them. Waldo saw the danger, kicked down the gate of his pigpen, ran to the kids, and pushed them out of the way just as the car slid right where they had been standing, saving their lives."

"That's amazing," said the city slicker, "But what happened to the pigs missing leg?"  Kyran said "I answered by scolding the city slicker.  I said, Mr., haven't you been listening to me about Waldo?  You don't eat a special pig like Waldo all at once..." There was one dinner when the talk became serious. Mark made a remark speculating one of the team might be the first draftee sent to combat in Vietnam. "My plan is to get a student deferment and stay in college until the end of the war."  Mark's remark angered one of the farm boys who shot back. "Monoly, I can't believe you'd be a draft dodger.  The rest of us are patriotic Americans and will serve our country if called upon.  We're not cowards running to Canada or hiding out in college." Before the emotions ran off kilter, Kyran took control of his young crew and calmed them.

"Boy's I've lived my whole life out here on the farm,

and that includes WW2 and the Korean War." he said and continued, "A few of your dads went to either or both wars and it disturbs me that anyone of you, someday down the line, might have to go off somewhere overseas and be in something as terrible as a war. I wish everyone of you could stay and live your complete lives out here on the farm where we live life at its best. Farm life is peaceful and fulfilling.

I sometimes think of myself and Alice as just another pair of plants growing on these 80 acres. We have our roots down and hold this land just like the wheat we grow. We hold it against the wind, the rain, or any unbenevolent event that God throws at us. Beyond our fence line is an enormous world that's full of terrible things. Our focus is here on this rich land. Alice and I pray for pleasant days and fair weather. We let all the rest beyond the fence lines be what it is. We'll worry about the planting, the harvest, and all we can control on our land. If it turns out at the end Mark," he said with a nod and a smile in Mark's direction, "That Alice and I were wasting our time driving the tractor to church, and we die only to discover there is no heaven, that will be OK because we appreciate each day on this farm and celebrate it here and now. I've seen lots of boys like you in summers past, all under this very tree, making all kinds of big plans for the future. For some, their dreams worked out, some didn't. But I hope everyone that's come to this good land took a handful of this farm with them, kept it in their pocket wherever life took them. I want you boys to keep a piece of this farm in your pocket, hold on to it forever. Breathe this fresh air, let the sun kiss your face. Feel this goodness."

Under the shade of a tall maple tree those summers long ago, the sun sparkling around us through the pointed green leaves far above our heads. These were excellent moments in our lives and linger in pleasant memories. This place is where we enjoyed the gentle summer breezes surrounded by green fields of grain, corn, wheat, and soybeans as far as you could see. When our eyes looked to the horizon, the rolling hills simmered from the summer heat. The warm summer air danced the dance of a Michigan summer afternoon. There we enjoyed our dinner conversation, food, and fellowship. Laughter would reach out into those growing fields, and in our hearts and souls we communed with nature. There we forgot about the world and all its complexities.

We were so different. Each of us ended up leading very different lives. But these were tribal gatherings, memorable times. Farming connected us. It brought us together in our essence. Life on the farm was twice as good as Kyran and Alice O'Conner described it.

On the last day of baling we gathered under the maple tree. It was payday. Kyran would have the checkbook out on the cherry-wood dining table brought outside one last time. He'd count everyone's hours up and write our paychecks. We earned a dollar an hour. It added up fast, our labor making us all prosperous on the farm.

# Chapter 5 *The Church Festival*

Molly, now distracted by her Pina Colada slurpee, requires more supervision as she drives. Every now and again I have to reach over to the steering wheel to correct her errant helmsmanship with a quick jerk as she wanders a tad bit too close to the center line of the road or off to the shoulder. And like always, she's fully engaged in the conversation, which so far has been more of a monologue on my part. But I can tell she's enjoying my reminiscing.

She is a well-practiced provocateur however, she grins and throws shade on my recollections saying, "Thank you Dad for not settling down in Carson City. I just can't imagine how boring your life was growing up, I'm soooo glad you and mom didn't raise me there."

"Boring?" I respond incredulously, "No way was it boring. Every day was full of fun. Occasionally there was some fabulous special event." "Like what?", she mocks, "The milk truck pulling into town?" She's in fine form and that's funny but she's definitely thrown down a challenge. I take a couple of minutes of silent recollecting until I sort through many splendid memories from my youth before deciding to share a happy elementary school memory. "The annual St.

Mary's Festival Molly, you won't believe how fantastic that was when we were little kids.

Bishop Babcock sent Father O'Brien to St. Mary's because he was a proven fundraiser, a money man. Father's job, after spiritual care, was to retire the enormous parish debt incurred when they built St. Mary's Hall in 1955. The magenta brick "Hall" was a gym with a stage, kitchen, and meeting rooms. The hall sat on a corner between the school and the rectory. It was a superb place for school plays, basketball games, weddings, receptions, banquets, and meetings. In fact, it was the only place in Carson City large enough for wedding receptions and banquets. However, it had cost over $100,000 to build and that was an incredible amount of money for a parish of about 400 adults, half of which were housewives, who today we describe with political correctness as stay at home moms.

In the early fall, just after the Labor Day weekend when most of the farmers completed harvest time, the weather would still be summer-like and perfect for holding St. Mary's parish's annual Church Festival. There were three principal events for the weekend. First, the women of the church cooked and served hundreds of chicken dinners inside the hall. Second, in a circus tent outside the hall, the men ran all kinds of money-making games for both kids and adults. The last event was the capper of the weekend; a drawing for the then fantastic amount of $1000.00 at the official close of the festivities on Sunday night. The purpose of the occasion was to raise money to retire the enormous debt on the Hall, but it did much more.

For us elementary school kids, it all would start on the Monday before the festival. That was the day the men in panel trucks would arrive to erect the giant brown circus tent. We elementary students at St. Mary's school would be on the lookout for them from across the quiet street. At the first recess we boys would rush over and ask the workmen if they needed any help. The men were always kind and patient with us boys, and they'd let us help. We'd pull on the ropes to help pull the tent up, they would let us swing the big sledgehammers at the wooden tent stakes. They would enjoy a moment of laughing when one of us skinny boys would topple over backward as we lifted those heavy sledges above our heads.

The men would playfully tease us about our budding manhood by saying, "You boys run over to school and send some girls back here to hammer down these stakes!" The wimpier we were, the bigger and more macho nickname they'd playfully give us. For a week we'd all have new names and answer to "Bruiser", "Muscles", "BrainBoy", and for Nocks who wore dark horn-rimmed glasses, "Bifocals." When recess ended, we boys would go back across the street to resume our school-day. It's a minor miracle that we never interfered in the men's work long enough to become a nuisance. Or maybe the men were too nice to complain.

When they finished raising the tent alongside the Hall, it was a magical transformation. It sharpened our anticipation of the upcoming festival, and the tent became a fun and fresh place to play for an entire week. The tent covering the sunny lot transformed our little world. The tent became a huge dark environment for all kinds of games we made up. We'd shimmy ourselves up the two inner wooden tent poles and touch the tent roof. When we were not playing a game, we'd be chasing each other around or be wrestling one another at the center of the big top. One rainy day we all went over at recess to the tent with our baseball gloves and played a baseball game inside the tent. We changed some rules to accommodate the two interior tent poles, the canvas roof, and the walls. Looking back on it years later as grown men, the former players would boastfully claim that history would show that we played the first indoor baseball game in Carson City.

On the Friday night before the festival, all the Catholic boys would ride our Stingray bikes to the Hall and help the adults with the last preparations and set up for the weekend. The women of the parish would be busy in the kitchen with stainless steel pots and pans clanging everywhere. The ladies would chatter among themselves and if they saw some idle kid in that kitchen, the ladies in charge would issue instructions and put that slacker to work. Regardless of your age, the women would find a task that needed doing. Even the dumbest kid in the parish knew these hard-working Parish women would make their life miserable if they didn't roll up their sleeves and pitch in.

The women were clever and resourceful. In the Spring they would deliver to each of the parish farmers a couple dozen chicks they got for free from the annual "peeps" giveaway by the local State Farm insurance agent. Over the summer the farmers raised the chicks to chickens and just before the festival, the men butchered the summer chickens for the main course at the festival. The local joke was if you wanted to know if one of the local farmers was Catholic, one could drive by a farm and if there were lots chickens running around, bingo.

The farmers also raised and donated what must have been a million fresh potatoes and carrots from small patches of land they reserved on their respective farms each year for the Festival. Potato and carrot peeling were tasks given exclusively to the girls; the women determined the boys were too mischievous to trust with sharp objects. Instead, boys were asked out to the tent to help carry the equipment needed for the games or carry and set up hundreds of folding chairs and tables.

A few months before the festival, the men of the parish who weren't farmers were also working diligently for its success. Father O'Brien assigned each man a large packet of raffle and chicken dinner tickets to sell. Father, not shy about using blunt force, would then use the Sunday Mass pulpit and the Church bulletin as media to report everyone's progress selling the tickets. This tactic insured there were no layabouts, even the worst performer bought at least a few raffle tickets and dinners if only just for their immediate family. The men who worked out of town connected to a network of supportive Catholics through the Knights of Columbus. They sold a lot of tickets through those relationships and those sales insured a steady stream of weekend Festival visitors from the nearby parishes.

The Festival would start at 10am on Saturday and end on Sunday evening, with the big tent and Hall making it weather proof. The Saturday meal crowd was a little less steady, but Sunday the line of people outside the Hall waiting for a meal continued all day. For us kids, the chicken dinners were not much of an attraction. We loved the action inside the tent.

The tent was packed with fun games, some for adults and some for kids. There was an 8-foot long silver horse's trough the parish men filled with water. An electric pump created a water current that went around and around the tank. Each year someone had a bunch of small plastic ducks with flat bottoms that they would put in the trough. The ducks would float around in a circle, and each kid could pay a nickel to fish one out with a net. Each duck had a number on the bottom corresponding to a prize. The top prize was usually a 1-foot tall stuffed bear, but most of us would end up with plastic spiders, rings, jewelry, whistles, rubber balls, balsa planes, bows and arrows with rubber tips, or those ping-pong paddles with the rubber ball and rubber band attached, known as paddle balls in those days.

The most intriguing game for us kids was the dice table. Even though it was straight up gambling, the parish allowed kids of any age to sit right there amongst the adults and shoot dice. The adults would play with quarters, half dollars, and to the amazement to us kids, even a full dollar. We kids were in with pennies, nickels, and once in a while we'd dare a dime. When we won a few cents, we beamed like flashlights, but when we lost the parish men running the game would sometimes need to comfort our broken hopes for making a quick fortune.

They would see our sad little faces and tell us we'd just bought a brick for the Hall. Somehow, those simple words made us feel a little better when they scooped up our coins and put them in the cigar box inside the booth. No one seemed concerned about kids gambling. The Church benefitting was the overriding consideration.

The last event and climax of the Festival was the raffle. Father O'Brien would use his bullhorn to gather everyone around and into the tent. There he'd brought the hopper full of raffle tickets from the Church vestibule, where it had been on display for weeks. Everyone at the Festival would come into the tent and wait to watch Father reach into the hopper and pull out the name of the winner. Almost always, the person who won wasn't present. Many times, the winner was an out of towner that no one knew. One notable exception was the year Mr. Tom McKenna won the grand prize.

Mr. McKenna was the home-grown Carson City hospital administrator, a retired Army Colonel who lost a leg as an advisor in Vietnam, a place we kids never heard of before. He was bespectacled with black horned rimmed glasses, thin with sharp features and jet-black hair. He looked every bit the accountant/administrator that he was. His skin was pasty white even though he worked a small family farm on the side.

When Father O'Brien happily announced over the loudspeaker he'd won the $1000.00 raffle, everyone let up a great cheer that echoed off the tent as he came up through the smiling crowd. People patted him on the back or shouted out to him to ask if he would buy a round with his winnings for everyone at the B and I Bar downtown after the festival.

Father greeted him with his great warm smile and shook his hand vigorously, thrilled that an honorable parishioner had won the grand prize. Mr. McKenna was smiling as he shook Father's hand but he refused the crisp $1000.00 bill that Father had been waving above his head. Mr. McKenna pulled Father in close to him and whispered something in his ear. Whatever he said, everyone could see Father's eyes mist up and the cheerful buzz in the crowd went silent.

Father O'Brien, his voice filled with great emotion and satisfaction, announced to everyone that Mr. McKenna had donated the prize back to the church. The reaction was electric with everyone yelling their appreciation by giving the loudest cheer we kids ever heard. Mr. McKenna seemed overwhelmed by the response, as everyone rushed up and surrounded him. Men reached over each other, patting his back or shaking his hand, everyone yelling compliments over the din of noise from the merry crowd of parishioners.

For us kids the most surprising and curious display of gratitude and affection came from the women of the Parish. All the ladies hugged and kissed Mr. McKenna enthusiastically on his cheeks and forehead, a display of public affections we children of the parish, and for that matter no one in this small rural community, ever saw before. Our eyes looked to our fathers and to Father, as we never saw our mothers act that way before. But seeing nods of approval from the temporal and spiritual authority figures, we realized this was pure and good. The ladies did their level best to leave lipstick prints all over Mr. McKenna's face. Everyone, including Mrs. McKenna, enjoyed his sheepish grin and embarrassment at the outpouring of affection.

The Monday after Festival the tent rental company men came and began taking down the great tent. In a few days it disappeared, and the only sign the festival happened was the trampled down brownish grass the great tent once covered. Soon the grass recharged and all traces of the festival disappeared for another year.

"You know Molly, occasionally I reminisce about that Church Festival. There's no better representation of community spirit. Over the years when I've encountered the common McKenna surname, I remember Mr. McKenna giving back that enormous amount of money. He set a fine example for all of us that day. His generosity demonstrated the nobility of character that comes with a commitment to a higher cause. We were lucky youngsters to grow up under the influence of people with these amazing small-town values." Molly rolls her eyes and replies "You're getting all mushy on me Dad, toughen up Buttercup!" I shake my head and laugh along with her. She can mock so well. I silently wonder if someday there will be a job market for her acerbic skill set.

# Chapter 6 *Boys State*

Molly continues driving our little red Jeep along an easterly route up and down the gentle rolling orchard fields to the west of Sparta. The cherry and apple trees stand in straight rows, shimmering with beautiful white and pink blossoms as short green spring grass grows underneath, the perfect place for finding Michigan's springtime delicacy, morel mushrooms. Twenty miles inland, the sky becomes cloudless and a beautiful deep blue; the sun sparkling off the pink and white blossoms. Everything in our sight is springtime fresh and growing. "I wonder Molly, is there anywhere in the world with more beautiful orchards than here in West Michigan?"

"Whoa, Whoa, Whoa, Dad", Molly responds, interrupting my comments on the beauty of the Michigan spring day that surrounds us, "Let's go back here a second, so you're telling me you and your hick pals were the first to play indoor baseball?"

"As the farmers I grew up among would say Molly, yes, that's a fact", I reply "My little hometown of Carson City is the historic site of the world's first indoor baseball game. That's amazing history, don't you think?"

She rolls her eyes, shakes her head and smiles the smile of someone who knows I played them. "Not going there Dad", she says after a chuckle and she turns the conversation back to a more thoughtful one. "Dad, I'm still not buying your story that being raised up in Farmville during the last century was such a big deal. It sounds pretty boring to me." In response, I suggest, "Let me tell you about my senior year in high school and I think you'll see it all differently." The idea brings out her best Mocking Molly "Oh Noooo", she moans spiritedly, "Not a whole year of old dad stories". "Too bad for you" I say, "But I've got you trapped in the Jeep and there's nowhere for you to run- HA"!

I begin my recollection. "Mark Monoly's detour from a simple rural high school experience started in the summer before senior year. Carson City's American Legion Post 420 selected and sponsored Mark to attend Boys State. The goal of Boys State was to gather boys identified as leaders from all over Michigan and bring them together to develop their leadership skills. They did this by giving them the goal of creating a model of Michigan state and local government, then run elections in a mock 2 party system. The Legionnaires held the annual event in late summer, a week before high schools in Michigan allowed football practices to begin. Every Legion Club in the state sent a high school senior they determined was the exceptional representative from their community. Michigan State University in East Lansing hosted the week-long event. When each of the 1,000 boys arrived, they assigned each of them to one of the faux political parties. During a week of meetings and organizational work, each party held conventions and nominated their candidates. The last day they held elections to fill every public office in Boys State of Michigan."

Mark and his folks arrived on the designated Sunday afternoon at the Brody Quad Complex, MSU's largest community of dormitories. Like all the other boys attending, they assigned him to a dorm room with a roommate, a boy named Mike Barrick from Adrian. After saying goodbye to their respective parents, Mark and Mike joined the rest of the Boys Staters at Jenison Fieldhouse for Boys State orientation.

American Legion officers conducted the orientation session. They laid out the basic plan. They predetermined each floor of their dormitories to represent a city. Every two floors of the dorms represented each one of Michigan's 81 counties.


Throughout the week the Legionnaires brought in guest speakers. The conferences featured select mayors from around the state. State representatives, senators, and Governor William Milliken held sessions too. Each politician described their experiences. Some talked about politics, others about policies and duties. All of them described the challenges of their respective offices.

The Legionnaires created a paramilitary environment at Boys State. They queued up the boys by "City" and marched them two by two to all meals and meetings. Every day started with everyone being marched to the flagpole for reveille in the plaza at the center of the Brody dorms. Before sunset they again lined everyone up and marched them to the flagpole for the lowering of the flag while taps played. Both morning and at night, the Legionnaires required each "City" to stand at attention in neat columns before the flag for reveille and taps. Every meal and meeting started with the Pledge of Allegiance and a patriotic prayer.

The American Legion had critics because of the militaristic way they conducted Boys State. The Legionnaires answered back that they designed the annual event to be an exercise in democracy. Legionnaires started the event 1934, so it they claimed it a tradition. But with the Vietnam War raging, the critics of the Legionnaires claimed that Boys State was a front to influence young men to join the military. The Veteran's flat out rejected that claim. They resisted calls to change their long-held traditions.

The week had its controversy. On the first morning Mark and Mike ate breakfast with a group of boys. The Vietnam war became a topic. Mike was the first to show his displeasure with the war. "I don't have a clue why they selected me to come here, back home I'm known as anti-war", said Mike "This is all military crap. I hate the war in Vietnam, I've organized protests in school." He could see his new mates nodding in agreement, the war was not popular with young men near draft age. Mike made a suggestion, "We should organize a protest here at Boys State."

Mark couldn't hide his sympathy, "I agree, we've got the nicest man in my hometown walking around with one leg courtesy of the Viet Cong. He's a member of my church, a decent man, but what did he lose his leg for?" he asked rhetorically. Then Mark answered his own question, "For nothing." The small group of boys at the table all nodded their heads in agreement. "What do you say Mark, do you think we can put together a group of Boys State participants and organize an anti-war protest?", Mike asked. Mark, making his first political choice of his life, looked around the table and answered "Will you guys join us?" Everyone agreed. "Then let's do it.", Mark said, "What do you all say to the suggestion that we take the full week here to organize as many guys as we can and hold the protest next Saturday at noon on the last day of Boys State. That way we'll be better prepared and the Legionnaires won't have time to kick us out or discipline us, we'll all be leaving for home. Let's assign guys to make handouts for the protest and surreptitiously distribute them to each room. We can spread the word among the attendees but kept it a secret from the Legionnaires. They'll want to shut down any antiwar activities." "Count on me", Mike replied, the others quickly agreed. "Let's meet every morning at breakfast, none of the Legionnaires will suspect a thing."

The next morning at breakfast Mark addressed the small group of conspirators, "What do you think about getting some coverage for the protest from the news media?" Mike responded, "Great idea Mark, an antiwar protest at Boys State will be newsworthy. The media can't ignore the irony of a conservative organization of military Veterans like the American Legion sponsoring a group of antiwar protesters. Let me reach out to the local Lansing TV stations and the Lansing State Journal, I'll inform them of the protest.

Everyone agreed. Mark continued and said "Let's contact them later in the week so the word doesn't leak back to the Legionnaires, I'm sure they'd try to stop us if they found out in advance." Everyone agreed with the plan.

Mark volunteered to get everyone who planned to attend the demonstration to bring an antiwar sign. He pilfered materials from the stock at each of the "party" headquarters, recruited a team to make them, then hid the signs in his room until the protest. At the specified time on Saturday, about half of Boys State came through Mark's room to pick up a sign on their way to met at the flagpole in the center plaza.

Mike had the audacity to borrow a bullhorn under false pretense from one of the Legionnaires. He stood under the flagpole with the bullhorn and lead the antiwar chants typical of the day "Hell no we won't go" and asking the growing crowd "What do we want" and the crowd shouted "Peace!" and Mike asked again "When do we want it?", and the answer came back in hundreds of unified voices, "Now!"

Through the bullhorn, Mike introduced Mark. "Mark Monoly is from Carson City and is here to tell you a little something about the war in Vietnam" and he handed the bullhorn to Mark.

"Thank you, Mike Barrick, favorite son from the city of Adrian. Thank you all for coming here today to express your opposition to the War in Vietnam. This senseless War has taken thousands of American and Vietnamese lives, all for nothing. Today we gather and say enough is enough, it's time to bring our soldiers home. None of us boys from Boys State should ever go to Vietnam. We have come here to Lansing to practice Democracy, it's past time to let the Vietnamese let Democracy decide their future, not the United States government forcing its will on them." The speech was short, but the boys all enthusiastically cheered Mark.

The protest caught the Legionnaires off guard and the protest was over before they found out it began. In contrast to past years when the event barely made any news, Mike's reaching out to the media proved very effective. Scores of reporters from TV, radio, and newspapers were there and they blasted the news of the war protest from East Lansing all across the state.


Within a few days the national television network news programs picked up the local feeds. The antiwar protest became known all over the country. It was by far the signature event of the 1969 Michigan Boys State.

After returning to Carson City from Boys State, it was traditional to invite the Boys State representative to the Legion Club member's dinner to report on his experience. Given the ruckus the protest made, the Vets were there in force, ready to listen to Mark describe his experience at Boys State. Mark held no illusions. He expected it would be like swimming in a pool full of sharks. The American Legion Club was 100% behind the men and women in uniform, no questions asked.

Civil War Veterans created the Carson City American Legion Post 420. Those vets pooled their money and bought an old two-story wood-framed house just off the main street in the late 1860s. The clubhouse was a typical small town American Legion Post and over the years vertical round steel beams replaced the downstairs interior walls to open the interior of the building. In the mid-1960s they built a sturdy cement block addition to house the bar, a few tables, a dance floor, jukebox, and a pool table. The original wood-framed house they used for storage, but for rare larger banquets and meetings, they dusted it off and used it again. For small meetings and banquets, guests sat between the steel support poles. There in the original section of the building, the vets gathered to hear Mark's describe his activities at Boys State.

There weren't any young vets in the club. The handful who'd served in Vietnam stayed away from the Legion, most had served their two-year hitch, including a year in Vietnam, then left the war and came home against it. There were a handful of women there, but the audience was predominately older men who'd served for the duration in WW2. A few wore the blue-striped pants, white shirt, and blue and gold Legionnaire's hats, but most came in street clothes. The air in the banquet hall had a blue haze from the many old soldiers who smoked. Normally gregarious, the group's mood that night was subdued. The men had seen the reports of the antiwar protest. It didn't sit well with them. To these loyal patriots, war protests undermined our troops in the field. Protesters were disloyalty personified. Some members said protestors were outright traitors.

After dinner Max Boyle, the Post Commander and high school shop teacher, introduced Mark. Mark could feel butterflies in his stomach as he came up to the podium to address the group of Veterans. All the men in the Club were his neighbors, fellow church members, and friends of his family. Mark knew they would be angry with him if he told them about his involvement with the protest.

Mark started by telling them, "Boys State was a great experience, I'm grateful for your sponsorship and I can't thank you enough. My political career got off to a bit of a slow start at Boys State. I ran for the office of county treasurer, but lost", and with a slight smile and a dramatic pause added "And to make the loss even harder to take, my opponent was some Larry Cadodee from Hubbardston." The men in the room never heard of "Larry Cadodee" before, but making fun of Hubbardston, a 600-citizen village in the local school district, was a good joke. They all smiled and chuckled a bit, enjoying a put down on a neighboring village. Mark continued saying, "I didn't give up with that one setback, I redoubled my efforts and I ran with great determination for a seat on the State Board of Education. I'm sorry to report that I lost that election too." he paused again, and with his eyes rolling in mock disbelief said, "To some kid from Crystal Lake. I thought I'd experienced the worst defeat ever losing to some Hubbardston kid, and then I lost to some Larry Cadodee from Crystal Lake!" The veterans all roared at the joke as Mark dramatically reached up and held his forehead while looking down at the podium, shaking his head and saying plaintively, "Man that hurt". The Vets roared with laughter at yet another poke at Crystal, an even smaller village in the school district and at Mark's comedic description his second failed election bid.

Mark saw he was winning them over and his butterflies disappeared. He continued, "But by now I'd caught an incurable case of political fever. One of my dorm roommates ran for the top job, he ran to become the Governor of Boys State, and I ran his campaign. I expect you all know of political patronage. Well, it was there alive and thriving at Boys State. My gubernatorial candidate promised to make me Chief of the State Police when he won. I thought to myself, what could be better than getting appointed as head of Michigan's law enforcement? Who knows, maybe I'd look great in that blue uniform. It turns out we won our party's nomination and I'm thinking about calling a tailor for that uniform, but, in the general election, we lost. This time to a kid from Detroit, which I can tell you feels a lot better than losing to someone from Hubbardston or Crystal Lake." Mark said in a lighthearted voice, and again the Legionnaires laughed and nodded their heads in approval of his speech.

Mark was at ease. He took one last dramatic pause as the last chuckled faded and then said "However, eventually I succeeded in my pursuit of high office. Because of the high esteem in which they held me, my new friends appointed me, for my beloved home county of Montcalm, to the high office of county dog catcher." Once again, the Veterans roared in laughter and applauded their support of Mark's experience at Boys State.

Mark's confidence and resolve resonated in his voice. He let the room go quiet and moved on to the heart of his presentation. He changed his tone of voice from lighthearted to serious. He made eye contact with each member before declaring, "There was another event at Boys State I'm certain you're aware of. I've come here tonight to tell you my involvement with it straight up."

Mark paused. His eyes moved across the room. He looked each Veteran straight into their eyes. Then he continued with a strong, serious voice, "You sent me to Boys State. I opposed the Vietnam War before you sent me and I have returned home unchanged." The room was in stunned silence, but the furious vets held their tongues. "I hope you respect me when I tell you I expressed my opinions at Boys State, and while there I exercised my right of protest, and my right of assembly. I was an organizer and participant of the protest against the war in Vietnam at Boys State and as you know, it made quite a stir". He stood there tall, calm, his head moving back and forth as he continued giving strong eye contact to each man in the room."

I helped organize and took part in those antiwar activities. I know this news disappoints many of you, maybe angers all of you. But I hope you all know it's not that I don't respect you, the truth is I value each one of you. It's not that I disrespect our troops in the field, the fact is I admire them. It's not that I don't love my country. I love my country so much I risk engaging your wrath. It is not my goal to anger you. You are the people I love and respect above everyone I know. But I want to change the path of destruction I believe we are on. This war, I hate it with all my heart.

It is my opinion, and it is my right to express my opinion, to say that this war is not America's war to fight. I turn 18 in a few weeks and I must, like many of you did, register for the draft. For my friends and myself, being drafted to fight in this war is a very real possibility. My generation is being forced to fight a war that we say is immoral. It is possible my friends and I could die in Vietnam, too young cast a vote, too young to buy a beer."

"To protest against this war, or protest against any issue that we choose, is a constitutional right. These American rights to disagree through free speech, assembly, voting, each of these rights you defended with your service. It is these freedoms I have exercised that you have borne arms to defend, and for which you declare your love of country."

"If I've brought attention to my generation's disapproval of this war while I was at Boys State, and if it helps one less American die for nothing, than I am proud to have done so. Many if not all of you disagree, but I want you to know how much I appreciate each one of you for your opinions, and I look up to each of you as a hero for your service and defense of our country. I trust you all and I pray that you do not question my patriotism nor love of country. We all have the right to disagree with each other, this is a fundamental essence of being an American."

Mark paused, looked down at the podium for a moment, and softened his voice and continued, "This summer a bunch of us were baling hay at Kyran O'Conner's farm. During lunch the Vietnam War came up while we all sat outside under the oak trees. Uncle Kyran couldn't solve the war problem, but I think he helped us by telling us what we all want. He said he wished all of us could come to the farm and live our lives between the fence lines. He said it's his comfort, there on the farm where there is a simple life of bounty from God. I love him for his wisdom. I want to leave that thought with you tonight.

We all have the same goals; we don't want any family to worry about their sons in war anymore. Like Uncle Kyran says, we all want to be on our side of the fence line, living good lives." Mark paused and looked around the silent and attentive room. Mark finished his talk saying, "I want to conclude my report by saying thank you. Thank you for your service to our country. Thank you for giving me this wonderful experience of attending Boys State."

There was dead silence as Mark made his way back to his table and sat down. It was dead quiet, not a throat clearing, not a cough, not a metal utensil scraping on a dinner plate. The silence that met Mark's speech was something to etch into memory. The room reeked of strong disapproval, but with an almost strict military discipline, the quiet also showed acceptance to the fundamental truths to which he spoke.

We knew Mark for his athleticism and likability, but in the presentation to the Legionnaires, he expressed his coming to adulthood with values, deep thoughts, and courage of conviction. One of us kids had taken these war Veterans, some of them decorated war Veterans, and asked them to rethink their values. A lot of those men there were the "America, love it or leave it types", but in one short simple speech, he convinced the Legionnaires to reexamine the principals Mark said they fought for. He got them to reconsider the values and lives for which they aspired."

News travels fast in small towns and the word on Mark's report to the American Legion club was mixed. No one changed their minds about the War in Vietnam. But the bottom-line scuttlebutt from the Legion Club was that it was hard to dislike Mark Monoly. The vets said he was tough; he was honest, and he was a real leader.

# Chapter 7 *Reverend Horace Clark*

Molly slows the Wrangler as we come to the crossroads at M37 outside of Sparta. "So that's the way it turned out Molly", I say, "Mark Monoly became an instant hero to us kids for protesting the War in Vietnam. We expected the Legion Club members to be mad at him. Many of them never forgave him, but he won their respect.

I tell her the war divided the country by the fall of 1969. Birth dates marked the dividing lines. "Don't trust anyone over 30" became a counter culture slogan. Mark had transcended that line, something the rest of us seemed unable to do with our parents and the older adults in the community. Mark grew from being just another kid in school to a popular persona. Every clique accepted him, and this student body was full of cliques. One might say he became the anti-Larry Cadodee." Molly teases, "You had enough kids to form cliques in Carson City?" "Oh yes." I respond. "At my high school the cliques came prepackaged."

I explain to her that the makeup of my old high school came from combining several small school districts into a larger merged district in the late 1950s. The resulting Carson City-Crystal Area Schools geographically became the largest school district in Michigan. It reaches 35 miles across in places.

Because of the distance between us, about a third of the kids we went to school with never saw the other two-thirds of their class during summer break. Everyone just lived too far apart. Each busload arrived at school with pre-made cliques. Kids boarded buses every day in the tiny villages that made up the school district; Hubbardston, Crystal Lake, Palo, Carson City, Sumner, Butternut, and the Catholic kids from St. Mary's Academy.

The large school district produced a disjointed, factional student body. The lack of a unifying element in the district affected many normal school activities. One challenge was the school's sports program, which presented all kinds of challenges.

Teams found it hard to put together any practice times during normal school hours or immediately after school. Kids living outside of Carson needed personal transportation to take part, and many families couldn't afford a second car. Special meetings or sports camps in the off-season just didn't happen, everyone lived too far apart. Coupled with the preexisting factions of the multiple communities, teamwork concepts didn't take hold. These factors combined and made the sports teams of Carson City Crystal High School possess one of the most dismal sports records of any school in the state. The Eagles just couldn't compete. The geography worked against the students. It disconnected us from each other and added to the many reasons the school lacked a uniting esprit de corps.

The class of 1970 started their senior year in school after Labor Day in September 1969, just like any other year. Students reported to the gym on the first day of school to attend the "Welcome Back to School" assembly. The seniors sat at the far end of the gym, the other classes in small regional groups. We Catholic kids sat together in two rows, boys in the front row and the girls in the back.

"Hey Brenna, wanna sit by me in history class this year so I can scope your tests?" teased Nocks. Everyone in earshot laughed at the thought of anybody being so desperate as to want to copy Brenna's answers on any exam, she struggled to get B's in any class. But she wasn't defenseless, she could be witty and she shot back, "Nocks you can copy me anytime you want but please remember not to copy my name on your exams like you did last year. That was a dead giveaway that not only are you a cheater, but it proved you're a dumb cheater." Brenna's unexpected sharp retort got a chuckle from everyone. Mark playfully slapped Nocks on the back and rubbed his head. "I've been creamed," Nocks deadpanned to the group's delight.

Mr. MacDonald was the high school principal and took to the podium on the portable stage at the other end of the gym, far from the seniors. He stood rigidly at the podium wearing a gray polyester suit and wide red paisley tie. MacDonald looked younger than his 45 years. He was short, on the pudgy side, and his flat top haircut gave everyone the visual message that he was a strict disciplinarian. He had a big-league scowl and used it without hesitation to quiet the gym. In a monotone voice he halfheartedly went through a boring list of details, school policies, hours, and the blah blah welcome back to school canned speech. It seemed like it took forever for him to get through his list of mandatories.

When he finally finished, he asked rhetorically, "Do you want to meet the new teachers?" Then things became much more interesting. One by one he introduced the new teachers, inviting them up from the bleachers to stand with him on the stage. It was like a beauty pageant. The new teachers stood onstage, lined up so everyone could look over the new talent.

He introduced the last new teacher, "A recent graduate from the University of Minnesota, I'd like to introduce Mr. Petterson. Mr. Petterson has a degree in English and the Humanities and will teach those subjects this year." Petterson got up from his seat in the bleachers and walked toward the podium. He looked like actor David Macullum who starred in the popular television show "The Man from U.N.C.L.E." He had fair skin and shiny blond hair complete with bangs, one of the few adults who wore his hair that stylish. He wore a fashionable dark 3-piece blue suit with a vest that seemed to advertise his superior literacy.

"Oh my God, look at him", Darby said before letting

out a loud, deep sexy moan she wanted everyone to hear.  All the girls giggled and Petterson, who visibly reacted to the moan, blushed as he walked up to the podium and shook hands with Mr. MacDonald. Darby's moaning got the rest of the girls to squeal as if he was one of the Beatles.  "OK girls, calm down", scolded Mr. MacDonald from the stage, "He's married you know."  Darby leaned over and staged whispered in a sly tone to our group, "Married yes, but happily?"

We saw Petterson's embarrassment from the swoons, but he showed a little strut in his stride as he walked to the stage.  His body language suggested he felt worthy of the squealing.  Mr. Petterson was the center of attention that day.  But the affections of young adolescents wasn't the only thing coming his way.

Mark turned around to the girls and threw his arms dramatically in the air and pleaded, "For crying out loud, what's Petterson got that I don't have?"  Darby, always the quick wit flashed back, "For starters, this girl's deep desires and fantasies."  Everyone laughed and once again the seniors drew the ire of Mr. MacDonald who reprimanded them saying, "You seniors need to be setting a better example over there."

When classes started, Mr. Petterson established himself as one of those teachers whom no student dared play for a fool.  He had a rare ability to command respect.  Not even the hardened troublemakers got far when they tried to test him.  He was serious. He was thoughtful. If it weren't for his striking good looks and youthful continence, he might pass himself off as a crusty old college professor. Passionate about the humanities, English, and literature, he communicated in each careful word he spoke. He challenged his students with every question he asked.

When students walked into his room, they knew they were there to learn. The goofy stuff a high school senior might pull, especially on a new teacher, got left outside his classroom door. He differed from the other teachers, well liked but not loved, respected but not feared. As the school year progressed, he took his classes through classics like Shakespeare and then into the more modern writers such as Faulkner. He loved to prod the students for their thoughts and opinions on any topic that came to mind, but he let none of his students repeat back what he characterized as "mindless dinner table fodder." He demanded that his students think and rationalize their thoughts. He insisted that his students articulate their thoughts in coherent, logical declarations. No matter what opinion anyone put forth, he'd challenge everyone to reason it out. Any of his students who didn't meet his standards he dismissed by declaring their proclamations as "not rational." For those students who were earnest about being their best, nothing was worse than to hear those words.

Mr. Pettersons problems came from Butternut. Butternut was a small village of about 25 homes on a railroad crossing 4 miles west of Carson City. Most of the Butternut residents and farmers from nearby attended the Butternut Reformed Church. The Catholic kids thought of them as hard scrabble Baptists, poor and ultra conservative. Darby described them with the put-down "That to be a member of the Butternut Church one either had to have less than 40 acres (we considered 80 acres the smallest needed to survive) or live in a house trailer."

Nothing exemplified the cultural divisions in the school system more than the Butternut Reformed Church. The school consolidation closed their rickety old one-room schoolhouse. But the merger usurped their unilateral authority and decision-making abilities. There must have been only 50 adults in that church, but for this school year they banded together and voted in the school board elections as a block. As a result, Reverend Horace Clark of the Butternut Reformed Church and two of his members won seats on the Carson City Crystal Area School Board. That gave the Butternut Reformed Church the controlling votes on the 5-member school board.

Reverend Horace Clark owned and operated the lone gas station in Butternut, his Church being too small to support a full-time pastor. The station wasn't on the main paved country road that passed through the tiny village. Instead, it was off along the abandoned railroad tracks on a dirt road 100 yards from the paved road. The gas station was a cooperative where the local farmers could buy their petroleum products at a discount and legally escape paying state road taxes if they stated in writing that the gas usage was in agriculture. Horace and the Butternut Co-op were the center crossroads of the community. Other than the church, it served as the main gathering place in the tiny village. It was the only business in the dinky one-horse town.

Clark, a tall and heavy man with slicked down salt and pepper hair, talked slowly with a deep baritone voice. He wore silver round wire-rimmed glasses and worked at the station in denim overalls and an oil-stained light blue long sleeve shirt. But when he came to school board meetings or to church, he always had on a nice-looking grey suit with a white shirt and black tie. He looked official and earnest. No one considered him an unpleasant man. At first, the concerns about his presence on the school board were minimal. No one outside of the few folks who attended the Butternut Reformed Church knew how ultra-conservative and controlling he and his cronies were to become on the school board.

Clark's educational attainment ended with a high school diploma. Known as a decent man, he was friendly and helpful to his neighbors. The son of a Butternut farmer, Reverend Clark preached passionately against the sins of drinking, smoking, and bombast'd what he called the lewdness of the times. He used the pulpit to preach against the general decline of morality caused by, according to him, popular music, television, and the movies.

Bob Petterson stood as the opposite of Horace Clark. A true liberal, Petterson personified sophistication and culture, and he stood out in Carson for having those qualities. He held a master's degree in humanities. Mr. Petterson, never seen in a church, described himself as an agnostic. Both men were likable, but we could describe neither one as being in the local culture's mainstream.

Mr. Petterson became one of the first adults in town to give a local voice of opposition to the war in Vietnam. He made a "rational" case against the war whenever the subject came up in his classes. His dispassionate arguments were very convincing. If a student justified the war by deeming it patriotic, Petterson's countered by asking that student "Are there any Viet Cong patriots? The answer is yes. Any person risking their life for a national cause is a qualifier for being labeled a patriot." Petterson reasoned further asking, "How can you say your support for the War comes from Patriotism? That's not rational. Patriotism is not a cause of war, it is the support of war. We cannot justify war by saying it's because we are patriotic, that is not rational."

Brenna once asked him, "My Dad and I got into an argument over the war and he said that I should love America or leave it. I told him I loved my country just the same as he does, but he didn't agree. What can I say to the "love America or leave it" people? What is the response?" "Ms. Brennan", he replied, "It might be best to ask a simple question, is America a diverse nation that protects and treasures free speech or is it a country reserved only for the people who agree with the war?"

Darby shared some details from her discussion with her dad, a decorated World War 2 veteran. "My dad says that the communists are trying to take over the world and we need to stop them." "Ms. Donahue," he challenged back, "Maybe you need a list of the countries communists took over by force of arms. I believe the total number is zero. Maybe you and your dad can define what America's vital national interests are in Vietnam? I believe you'll find there are none. If there are no national interests in Vietnam, then the rationale for continuing war becomes insupportable."

Mr. Petterson challenged us to respect the opinions of others. He demanded students defend their opinions with logical arguments. He'd work over offenders so hard he'd have them spinning in their chair. Petterson's challenges brought out our young minds first cognitive adult opinions, regardless of his opinions on the chosen topic. His challenges to the "opinions" brought to school by the students from Butternut got back to their homes. Petterson's methods of calling for logic over beliefs did not please Horace Clark and his cult followers. Petterson's Socratic methods became the undercurrent of displeasure Clark and his followers began to voice about Mr. Petterson.

Mr. Petterson assigned a Pulitzer Prize nominated book for his seniors to read for his American Literature class. This novel, "Henderson the Rain King" by Saul Bellow, ranked as the 21st best on critics lists of the greatest novels in the English language. The National Association of Humanities Teachers recommended the novel for high school students. The English Department used that respected group as a source for selecting reading material for the school's students.

A passage in "Henderson" became the center of controversy in the school district. In the book, his friends shave all the hair off the drunken main character and leave him alone and naked on a beach. Petterson, the Minnesota Liberal, said it was a harmless fiction. When they heard about "Henderson", the newly elected Horace Clark faction of the school board said it was a dirty book.

The school board called Mr. Petterson to a meeting to explain why he assigned "Henderson the Rain King" to his senior class. They met in the high school library where they pulled large rectangle shaped tables together for the five board members, superintendent of schools, high school principal, three middle and elementary principals, and the typical handful of school parents attending the meeting with grievances to air. Men comprised the membership of the Carson school board. Everyone dressed for official meetings wearing suits, white shirts, and ties.

The board invited Mr. Petterson to come to the head table along with the board members.

Horace Clark, the black grease under his fingernails belying his otherwise proper looking Sunday best gray suit, started his no-nonsense inquiry.  With his slow and deliberate deep voice, he began, "Mr. Petterson, the board thanks you for coming to the school board meeting tonight.  It's been brought to our attention by an alarmed and concerned parent that the choice of books you assigned to our young and impressionable students is not material that is proper.  Can you comment                 on                 this?"

Mr. Petterson, a man born with the polished skills of a diplomat, smiled and answered. "First, I want to thank the school board for their continued support and interest in the school English department.  I am here in my first year of teaching.  It surprised me when the school administration appointed me the English Department chairman.   But I'm honored they appointed me chairman and the team is doing the best     we     can     do     for     our     students.

Last summer in my capacity as Chairman, I tasked our English teachers to develop the guidelines for selecting suitable reading materials for our students. After much discussion and research, the teachers recommended using the guidelines from The National Association of Humanities Teachers.   Most high schools   use   these   time-tested   standards.    The group's   decision   to   use   these   benchmarks   was unanimous. This resource became the filter from which we selected proper reading material for the children of our school district."

"Mr. Petterson, can you assure us this group of whoever they are, are not conspiring to corrupt the Christian morals of our youth?" Petterson's reserve left him for a second as a look of bewilderment came across his face. In a heartbeat he regained his composure and answered, "I'm sorry Mr. Clark, we are a public school. We don't teach religion here. I think it's safe to assume all teachers genuinely want to improve the lives of our children. No one wants to ruin them."

Clark chuckled sarcastically and nodded to the other members of his group on the board and said, "Well Mr. Petterson, all I can say is that we have parents who object to this material. I trust these parents' judgment on the proper material, not this "National Group." I've never heard of them. We are raising a generation of kids these days who are disrespectful, immoral, and downright rebellious.

For example, take that young Monoly boy and the way he acted at Boys State a few weeks ago. His behaviour is a prime example resulting from an impressionable young man who reads immoral literature. His behavior concerns us. I am asking you Mr. Petterson to review each of the books you are using as teaching materials for this year. We want you to remove any that do not meet our community standards. Please come back to the school board meeting next month and give us your report. Let's put this episode behind us."

The polite smile left Petterson's face. He said, "Mr. Clark, I understand young Mr. Monoly exercised his freedom of expression and then became a perfect example of how to be polite and respectful when one disagrees with others." Before Mr. Petterson could finish his remarks, Clark interrupted and said, "The board needs to move on to the next item of business." The initial discussion defining which reading materials were proper for students in our school ended abruptly.

## Chapter 8 *Noodles*

Molly slowed the Jeep as we hit the outskirts of Sparta, a town of 3,000 where the local claim to fame is agriculture and big-time high school football. Sparta lies in the low rolling orchard hills north of Grand Rapids, Michigan's second largest city. Sparta is a long, narrow borough with railroad tracks crossing the main road near the granaries on the east end of town. The city limits sign greets us with subtitles underscoring the 6 years the Sparta Spartans won state championships.

"Why is Sparta always so good in football Dad?", Molly asks as we tool our way through downtown Sparta, hitting each of its three stoplights. "Good question Molly, it's triple the size of Carson City, so it's grossly unfair that they play in the same league in sports, but in most other regards Carson City and Sparta are similar small towns. Sparta's football teams always win the league, they're always a force in the state football playoffs. It's been that way since I can remember. Some schools consistently produce a winning football team" I said. Molly teases, "So, they beat Carson City on a regular basis, huh, Dad?"

"Well, yes, but everybody beats Carson regularly in every sport, it's the sad but simple truth," I reply, "But Carson City hasn't been a loser every year. You want to hear my story about that?" "Oh no, not another interminable boring story about how you and your farm boy pals got good in sports by riding cows to school?" she says in her best mocking tone. I reply, "Molly, you sure know how to fire up a storyteller."

Carson City had a record of losing in every sport, and not just to Sparta. But the locals expected our class of 1970 to be the exception to the legacy of losing. They extolled us early on as being special not only in sports but also in our studies. We grew up hearing our class would be the best in everything.

The expectations started years earlier. Our little league baseball teams showcased our athletic talent, and even then, the speculators said when we reached senior high school, we'd win championships in every sport. We heard it from parents, teachers, and from the owners of the small shops in town. Whenever as little kids we scraped a couple of nickels together for a moon river coke, the patrons at the Bamboo Room, one of three small restaurants in town, would give words of support to our athletic exploits. They raised us up and us convinced our future sports achievements would be amazingly successful. They had the same expectations for our academic endeavors.

In the Junior year for the class of 1970, the football team had been competitive in their football games but came up a point or two short in every game but one. The team finished the season with a disappointing record of 1 win, 1 tie, and 6 losses.

Small town athletes dread losing because it can brand one a laughingstock for life. The junior year football experience disappointed everyone. When the team fell flat on its face, it became known as the thud heard around the town. But our upcoming senior season gave us a last chance to defy the odds and have a winning season. Before the season began, hopes were again high for our group. Everyone expected a long waited for championship.

It is frustrating in football to lose games. It's heartbreaking to lose close games. Every football game produces a week of bumps and bruises. Practice times are the same for winning and losing. When a team wins a game, they savor the special magic of winning in football. The physical aches and pain become easy to bear. Nothing is more gratifying in sports than winning a football game. It is the best experience in any sport. But in Carson City, building a winning team is difficult to do.

Carson-Crystal Area Schools is best described as a school district with limited resources. Our school didn't have a weight room, weights, or any off-season conditioning programs. The start of football practice began in the second week of August. Each player pledged to work himself into football playing condition for the fall. Without off-season programs, boys trying out for the team failed to understand what it took to get into a competitive physical condition to play football.

Competing schools had weight rooms. They organized extensive summer training programs. In contrast, Carson boys believed a few sessions of jogging made up an off-season conditioning program. The lack of off-season programs in Carson, with none of the other mitigating factors, would explain the long history of losing.

But for the 1969 football season, everything changed. On the Friday before the first practice in mid-August, everyone trying out for football came to school for scheduled physicals and to pick up their football gear. Mark called an early "players only" meeting, something no Carson City athlete ever did before. After the physicals ended, the team met in the high school band room.

It was a surprise when Mark called the meeting. Until that moment, team leadership never interested him. Before he was a go-along, a non-standout in the crowd. After Boys State, he started acting on his natural leadership abilities. His experiences at Boys State gave him newfound confidence.

Mark stood before the team and began the meeting saying, "Guys, you remember last spring when we got together and agreed to develop small groups of workout teams. Seeing so many of you today for the first time since spring, I can tell you did a great job working out. Every player kept their commitment to the team. I promised you last spring if you worked hard, I'd give you a guarantee this fall. Here it is, on my word, we will not lose a single football game this year." That statement of confidence hit everyone like a Michigan thunderclap. Never had we heard anyone make that kind of promise."

"I know keeping a commitment to work out wasn't easy for any of you," he continued, "You guys who live on the farms worked out alone, and that's amazing. Everybody sacrificed to make us better. Nocks took the entire summer off from the carney shows with his family to work out and be with us. Everyone worked hard and that's the reason we're going be champions this year, right Nocks?" With that Mark glanced at Nocks who stood up to take a turn addressing the team.

"That's right," Nocks said, "Let me tell you about the Larry Cadodees in my group. They're a little crazy. After workouts at my house we'd put on swimsuits and head up to Crystal Lake for "Sauna Time!" We jumped in the car and rolled up the windows and turned the heater on full blast. We'd drive up to the lake, nobody died of the heat but I can tell you seriously man, we came close a couple of times."

"We agreed that the first guy to say the word "hot" had to buy the cokes at Lonnie's Drive Inn after the swim. Know what? Nobody ever gave in. The car reached up to a million degrees hot too. How about that for being Carson Tough?

When we'd get to the lake, we raced across the street to the beach, and kept running way out into the water. It's a good 100-yard sprint to get to the deep water and I hate to tell you, despite my being a powerful sprinter, I never beat anybody to the deep water the whole summer." Declaring himself a powerful sprinter drew loud hoots from the team. By far, Nocks was the slowest man on the team. Nocks grinned and shrugged his shoulders and continued, "But I think we developed a good power high step to bring into football because of that daily race."

"You guys from out-of-town may have read about it. Somebody mentioned our daily mad dash in the Carson City Gazette in the "Coming and Going" section. They said we were racing daily for this year's football championship. I agree."

Mark took back the podium. "One last thing, we have the athletic code kicking in at the start of our first practice. The number one thing I want you to know is that Nocks and I will hunt you down like a dog if you break the code. Remember, no drinking or smoking during the season. The number two thing is Nocks and I got our hands on a keg of beer and tomorrow night we're inviting you guys for the last grasser of the summer. For you guys who aren't Catholic, I'll tell you, this is how we start Lent, we blow off a little steam before we get serious." The team laughed and clapped. Mark ended the meeting by lifting his hand up to get everyone's' mind back on football and said

"It starts Monday guys, and this year, our opponents, especially Sparta, will find out we are tough enough. Together we will handcuff lightning and throw thunder in jail."


That Saturday night, as promised, The Nocks and Mark got everyone together in a secluded county park west of Crystal Lake. They held the typical grasser with cars parked in a circle out of sight from nearby roads. They built a small fire in the middle of the circle of cars, had every car's FM radios tuned into the same radio station. The Rolling Stones "Honkey Tonk Women", The Temptations "I Can't Get Next to You", Bobby Sherman's "Little Women", Three Dog Night's "Easy to Be Hard", "Harry Nilsson's "Everybody's Talkin", and other popular tunes played on into the late summer night. Every one of the players came. A few brought a date, others came with their sweethearts, a few brought non-football playing friends.


The partiers drank ice-cold beer from the pony keg, smoked cigarettes, told crude teenage jokes, and pulled pranks on each other. A few make out sessions occurred before curfews kicked in to disperse the partygoers. As the Coming and Going section of the Carson City Gazette described a proper social gathering, "a good time was had by all." Football practice started on Monday, so did the athletic rules. This last grasser of the summer meant no one could get ejected from sports or school since neither had officially started. Pre-season grassers were low-risk and high fun.

Football practice started the following Monday, and the full complement of 26 players showed up. Each player came with a new set of muscles gained from the summer workouts. The training paid off for every participant, except Nocks. He attended every session but failed to progress. When other guys started at ten weightlifting repetitions and built up to forty or more over the summer, Nocks struggled to hit ten reps in any of the workouts. Despite attending every single session, he showed up on the first day of football still being on the chubby side. The summer workouts earned him no noticeable physical improvements.

Despite the lack of development and having virtually no athletic skills, Nocks remained a favorite on the team. He was affable to a fault. Nocks flashed a quick smile and laughed well at every opportunity. But no matter how hard he tried, he never made himself into an athlete. The Nocks made up for his athletic deficiencies by being the "holler guy." He became the loudest and most vocal player on the team. We thought of him as all bark and no bite. None the less, Nock's hard work and popularity earned his way onto the team."
Nocks had feared his athletic shortcomings and lack of progress in the off-season training program would cause him injury at the hands of his teammates. "Mark turned himself into an animal. He's gonna cream me every day in practice" he'd say to anyone

on the team. "If not Mark, look at all you other guys, everyone is as tough as nails, everyone except me."

The toughest guys on the team belted everyone else around all season long in practice. Nocks was on the other end of the spectrum and secretly, everyone agreed to go light on him in practice so he didn't get hurt or quit. No one expected Nocks to be cut from the team either. The coach liked Nocks as well as the players, plus with only 26 players, Coach Noodles didn't have many extra guys.

Chuck "Noodles" Cadwell, a balding 45-year-old Pennsylvania native who somehow ended up in Carson City, took the unenviable job as head football coach of the Carson City Eagles. Legend had it the nickname came from his doting grandmother who picked him up as an infant and dubbed him "My cute little Noodles." A real football coach coming to Carson City wasn't unlike someone driving to the middle of Death Valley to go ice-skating. The team scuttlebutt had it he didn't get any job offers anywhere else, so he sucked it up and became our head coach.

He was a football coach deep down to his Pennsylvania Dutch bones. Being an underpaid high school math teacher was his means to the end. Noodles had to compete to recruit players in Carson's small pool of athletes. There weren't a lot of players good enough to play multiple sports, so all the coaches competed for the best athletes for their respective teams. Around the school and in his classroom, Noodles put his arm on every kid to recruit them for football. He would tell them what an exceptional football player he could become, what glory they would win in football. If the kid resisted by voicing a lack of interest or he played other sports, Noodles would scooch up his nose and say "Really" in his most lighthearted and condescending tone.

Noodles saw that Mark Molony's class possessed good speed as a group had enough talent to win. He didn't know that Mark had created a team workout program for the summer so Noodles put together a once a week soccer program. He saw from the soccer games that although the players didn't have any proper football size; the boys displayed quickness and good hustle. Based on that observation during the summer Noodles designed the team's defensive strategy based on the speed of the team. He planned to exploit the team's collective speed to out-finesse and run past bigger and stronger teams.

He used the pro-set defense when no other high school coach did. His design used the pro set of four linemen, four linebackers, two cornerbacks and one safety. Most other teams used five linemen and three linebackers, but by using the two tackles to pinch and keep linemen from coming out and blocking the linebackers, offenses couldn't figure out how to counter. He put his speediest players in at the linebacker positions where they would be free to run. Every practice he worked with the players on techniques, based on their speed, that would disrupt any opposing offense from scoring.

At every practice Noodles wore football cleats, white crew socks and short-cut white football pants, same as the team, and a grey "Eagles Football" t-shirt. As part of his teaching methods, he would sometimes take a player's position in practice to demonstrate how plays worked. The team would be in full pads with helmets strapped on tight. When the coach took a player's position in full tackle scrimmages, no player dared hit him. He didn't wear protective padding plus, in the eyes of us teenagers, he was an old, fragile man.

In the last day of practice before school started, it rained a monsoon type rain. But we practiced anyway. Noodles decided it was a good day for one of his teaching by participation moments. He lined up as the quarterback to demonstrate a technique for running a sweep with an option play. The gimmick that made this play work came from the quarterback's ability to show an effective series of fake hand-offs to running backs. After faking the defenders out of position, the quarterback would run the ball around the end and up the field. Noodles' special talent of faking the hand-off, we'd tease him, came from his nicely sized potbelly he used to hide the ball.

Coach Noodles called the play in the huddle, lined up over the center, barked out the signals, and took the hike. He spun around to fake a couple of hand-offs before rolling out on a sprint, well, for him a sprint, to the outside. His face lit up. He relished the action, perhaps reliving some old glory football memories as he ran around the defensive end into the wide-open flats. He chugged along in his clean gray t-shirt and the spotless white football pants, spraying a little mud up behind him. He ran wobbly past the defensive linemen and turned up the field for what looked like a sure touchdown. We knew when he scored, he'd taunt the defensive practice team for the rest of the week.

The Nocks never saw much game time on the team, but with so few members on the team he played defensive tackle as the mock opponent team. His football acumen hit the scale somewhere next to nonexistent. Nock's roly-poly personality was the opposite of the aggressive intensity normally found in a football environment. He couldn't change from his easy-going personality to the attack mentality football players require.

Nock's extra weight made him a step slower than his teammates. His real contribution to the team came from his being the "holler guy." No one on the team ever came close to even matching his effervescent verbal enthusiasm. The Nocks would lower his normal voice and would boom out all the clichés, guttural utterances, and Coach's football sayings from the sidelines in every game. His voice became the heart of the team's unbreakable spirit. He kept every team member's enthusiasm at the highest level. The players and coaches all loved him, and he loved being on the team, but as hard as he worked, Nocks didn't have it in him to be a football player.

As Noodles rolled out of the pocket and got his 45-year-old body rumbling along as fast as he could go, Nocks came after him from his usual position, playing against the number one offense as a defensive tackle. On this one play in practice and for the only time in his lackluster football career, The Nocks found a great sudden surge of speed, power, and quickness.

When the center hiked the ball, The Nocks dodged out of the way of his blocker. He sliced into the backfield at the perfect right angle and led the chase of Noodles. The coach turned the corner and avoided being tackled. With his old man sprint he started to breakaway, but instead of scoring a touchdown, he got a little surprise.

Nocks came out of nowhere and dove at him, about a foot off the ground. Nocks hit the mud and slid forward, and with one arm reaching out, he grabbed Noodles' back foot. The old Coach went flying out of control and smashed headfirst into the mud. The spectacular shoestring tackle put Noodles into a slide. He slid a good ten muddy yards on the side of his helmetless head.

For that one play The Nocks forgot the prime unwritten rule in football; never tackle a coach. The rule is especially true when that person is the head coach. Noodles, who after being on the wrong end of this fantastic tackle, laid on the ground for a moment covered with black mud from head to toe. He jumped to his feet and slammed the ball to the ground with a splat, holding his bleeding ear and in obvious pain he screamed "Gusnocki, what in the hell is wrong with you?" Nocks looked up sheepishly at the muddy and bloodied Noodles after making the greatest, dumbest tackle any of us ever saw.

At first, we were all concerned that Noodles' got hurt. As soon as we saw there were no serious injuries, we couldn't hold back any longer. The whole team broke out laughing hysterically at the whole comic event. Everyone except Nocks. He stood next to Noodles, both covered in mud. Nocks couldn't understand why the coach was so mad. We'd witnessed the most spectacular, but not very smart, tackle of the century. As a result, on the first day of school in the fall of 1969 Coach Noodles Cadwell showed up with a cauliflower ear, skinned nose, and black eye all courtesy of our pal Nocks.
30 years later Noodles would still retell the incident. He'd laugh and ended his recollection of the story by shaking his head and rolling his eyes. All while saying with the same exasperation as if Nocks had just tackled him again saying, "That damn Gusnocki."

Carson's players looked forward to the two-a-day preseason practices. The extra pounds of muscle on each player created newfound enthusiasm and a point of unification for the team. But the first day the team's solidarity got tested. A player from Hubbardston, Doug Kennedy, who we hadn't seen all summer, showed up with hair newly grown down to his shoulders. Noodles, a crew cut man himself, pulled Kennedy off the field and gave him the word.

"Kennedy, we don't have room on the team for hippies and war protesters," he said to Kennedy in front of the entire team. We all thought his hair was cool. The rest of our parents limited boys' hair length to the middle of the ear. Hair length had a status with us. Long hair symbolized opposition to the Vietnam War. Nobody's parent's in the school district allowed hair that long except Kennedy's. Doug didn't want to jeopardize playing football and he pleaded his case to Coach Noodles. "It's only hair coach, it's not stopping me from playing football."

"The hair is gone before school starts or you're off the team" Noodles shot back. Doug wanted to play football. For the second football practice that year, he came in with his hair cut down to the maximum allowed length. Doug didn't want to be a distraction to the team goals. He decided to comply with the rules. To his credit, Doug turned the negative into a positive by declaring everyone on the team owed him 100% effort for the locks he'd given up for them. We all respected him for putting the team first, and Doug's hair sacrifice made him one of the leaders on the team.

Molly kept the Jeep on its steady easterly course. As we left the gently rolling hills of West Michigan, they gradually wore down to become the flat plains of Central and East Michigan. "You know Molly, I don't think I had a better experience growing up as I did on that football team. Football just might be the ultimate team sport, 11 guys with a specific task to do on every play. If one guy doesn't come through and execute his assignment, it ruins the whole play. But our team had a ton of factors working against us before we even put on the pads. Those factors were unique to our school and they made winning nearly impossible.

The geography of the school district and its awful sports history worked against the football team in the fall of 1969, but we fought through the grim history to build a united, winning team. Overcoming these obstacles was an incredible accomplishment. To this day, everybody from that team carries a special feeling and high self-confidence born from that football team's experience. We fought through the schedule and became an elite team and high drama came when the season got down to the last game. It was the biggest game of our lives.

With one game to go, the Carson City Eagles football team found itself the darling of every high school football fan in Michigan. The Eagles came into the ultimate game of the season undefeated and unscored upon. People all over the school district rose up and became rabid followers of the team's success. With every win, the football players became increasingly popular local celebrities.

Coach Noodles turned down a flood of interview requests from reporters from every media outlet in the state saying he was too busy coaching the team. Mr. McDonald, following school board instructions, took those interviews and became known as the "Highest Flying Eagle." The season climax had an extra interest in part because of Carson's tradition of having homecoming on the football season's last game.

A few days before the big game, the Carson City Gazette published a full front page on the football team, the first time the paper ever headlined a sports team. One of the articles contrasted the team's success to the past dismal football history by highlighting the Eagles star running back Tim Fitzgerald. The article pointing out that Tim's dad was on the last Carson football team that had won a homecoming game.

To cap off the excitement, Sparta was the homecoming opponent coming into the game with a state record 55 game winning streak. Despite the Eagles perfect record, Sparta was the heavy favorite to win.

The Sparta Spartans had more students than any school in the conference. They ranked as a class B school system. All the other schools in Carson's athletic league ranked either a smaller class C school or even a D. Rather than compete with schools their own size in the Grand Rapids area just 10 miles south of Sparta, they made long bus trips north where their school size would be a distinct advantage. Their star player, Dwight Lowery, son of district court judge Dwight Lowery Sr., scored over 20 touchdowns during the season and was heading the following year to play for Michigan State University on a full scholarship.

Sparta expected to win another routine championship. Their expectations for their team success was always high. One of the most a well-known football powerhouses in the state, all the radio, newspaper, and the local TV station's "experts" picked Sparta Spartans to beat poor hapless Carson City in an easy cakewalk. The Grand Rapids Press labeled Noodles Cadwell's team as "Cinderella Carson City" during the season. In a preview of the championship game, the paper drew the ire of Carson fans by predicting Sparta would turn Cinderella Carson City's homecoming float back into the "bumpkin's pumpkin." The insult didn't dampen the hometown enthusiasm for Carson City-Crystal High School's homecoming celebration. The effect was the opposite, it fueled the excitement.

Carson traditionally planned homecomings for the last game of the season so as not to interfere with harvest time. Instead of working on the farms, students were free to participate in the traditional homecoming events. The 4 high school classes sought and borrowed generous farmers flatbed wagons upon which they built floats for the homecoming parade. Farmers who loaned wagons also got the small-town honor of pulling the float with their tractors in the parade.

Everyone expected this homecoming's attendance to be a record setting. To raise money for the floats, each class went all out with bake sales, dances, and candy sales. The seniors got an old junkyard car and set it up on a vacant lot on main street and sold tickets for fifty cents each for three swings with a sledgehammer to smash the car. It was a popular spot for kids and adults alike to vent hostilities or to impress their friends.

In past years it wasn't uncommon to see an unfinished float in the parade. In those years's homecomings became more like wakes for failed football seasons. It was common for a prankster sneak a "R.I.P." message on a float to serve as an exclamation point for yet another miserable season of football.

But the 1969 homecoming experience brought on a fresh enthusiasm. No one could remember a year when each class finished their float on time for the parade. More impressively, each entry looked sharp. Every class kept their design and location secret to discourage the vandalism of past years. The pranksters took the night off, a clear show of respect for the high-flying football team. The community's focus was clear, beat mighty Sparta.

With the flag bearing honor guard from American Legion Post 420 leading the way, the homecoming parade started down a closed off Main Street at dusk on a cool and cloudless Friday night. Each of the high school classes found the coolest car in which their respective class officers rode in the parade. The freshmen got a brand-new shiny Camaro from Geller Chevrolet, the sophomores got Burns Funeral home's black Lincoln hearse, which was pretty cool given their float theme was "Dig It", a reference to a graveyard for Sparta Football. Helen Flanagan drove the junior class representatives in her long-dead husband's jet black 1934 Chevrolet DA Master. She rarely brought it out of storage and into the sunlight, so her car rolling down main street made the parade extra special. The seniors borrowed Dr. Brennan' s classy bright blue Cadillac Eldorado.

Although Dr. Brennan owned the city's only Cadillac, a smattering of residents owned cool cars. The inventory included antique cars, convertibles, and lots of muscle cars. The owners of these cars were delighted to let students borrow their prizes for parade service. These cars carried football players, cheerleaders, and whoever local public sentiment considered a hometown celebrity. People like Father O'Brien, the Mayor, or the local cub scout troops rode in these special automobiles.

Most of the parade entries tossed penny candies to kids along the route. Savvy moms with young ones attended the parade at its starting point on the corner of Maple Street and M57. On the north east corner of the road stood Brooks Grocery store. The cinder block building butted right up to the side street and yielded zero standing room. Across the side street on

162

the west side was Helen Murphy's side yard. The kids in her yard got the candy thrown from the floats because there would be no competition from the older, quicker, savvier kids. Over the years, moms with young ones had figured out the candy typically ran out somewhere along the route, and the unwritten small-town parade code of conduct was implicit. Simply put, only the youngest kids could use Helen Murphy's front yard. There they could candy up in a kinder, gentler race for the sweet handouts in contrast for the free-for-all that happened with the older bonbon hooligans further down the parade route.

Homecoming in 1969 was the longest parade in memory. An enormous crowd turned out to watch. It was a memorable year, not only in sports, but the high school and middle school bands could even play recognizable tunes. For the school's band director, the bands ability to play music well was an accomplishment, not an annual guarantee. The last entry of the parade was the Carson City volunteer fireman's truck. They pulled a handful of lucky kids out of the crowd at the start of the parade and let them ride in the truck. The kids literally had a blast blowing the polished red firetruck's sirens and horns intermittently during the march across town.

The football team changed the culture. With each win, merchants in Carson City, Crystal, and Hubbardston all painted their storefront windows with supportive messages like "Undefeated and Unscored Upon" or "Eagles Soaring." Mark Monoly had painted

163

the football team's unusual mantra "If They Don't Score, We Don't Lose" on Flanagan's Clothing Store window. Every car radio antenna in the district sported a pair of blue and gold pompoms.

Football team members became celebrities. Their fame grew to a climax for homecoming. When a player or their parents entered a local business, the patrons and the owners showered them with attention. It was especially gratifying when a team member got that treatment in a village where they didn't live. Those warm welcomes and encouraging remarks were heartfelt and unifying. Good wishes from virtual strangers came to the players through their association with teammates from outside their own tiny village. The locals knew the positions they played and each individual's football accomplishments. It seemed like the school district grew into one small town.

# Chapter 10 *Kickoff*

Molly deftly passed a slow-moving car. She breezed past it and returned to her favorite pastime, mocking me. "You're telling me that homecoming was the height of the social season in Carson City?" "Ahhh, well,", I reply when it hits me how important high school homecomings are in sleepy little villages like the one I grew up in, "That's not too far off from being true. In small towns such as Carson City, daily life is quiet. What breaks the quiet are the annual traditions like homecoming where everyone in town turns out for the celebration. Everybody knows someone who's planned or taking part in the parade, and those relationships always guarantee a good turnout, although the football game after was less of an attraction.

In earlier years, hardly anyone attended home games. Maybe 50 people went, never enough to fill the three sets of green wooden bleachers on the home field sidelines. But Carson City's magical 1969 football season was coming to an exciting finish. It looked as if the entire population of the town joyfully followed the last parade entry, Carson's volunteer fire department. The firefighters hung all over the red pumper, waving to friends and neighbors as they passed by. The truck came slowly down Main Street to its destination, the parking spot behind the goalpost of the football field behind the school.

This football team's season was the complete opposite from the countless failing teams in Carson's history. With each of 1969 team's amazing wins, the crowds grew larger at every game. For the first time, the homecoming game, not the parade, was the star of the evening. The football field's bleachers filled and the crowd was six people deep all the way around the gridiron. The Carson City Gazette estimated that 3,500 people attended the game, an incredible number for this town of 1,000 residents. It was, by far, the largest crowd ever to attend a football game in the school's history.

There was an exuberant anticipation in the air that cool autumn night. The glaring lights from the wooden telephone poles high above Carson's football field bore down on the dew sparkled green grass. They illuminated the short grassy hills that formed the hollow on the visitor's side of the field. The glare of the lights stretched out to the endless rows of harvested corn stalks that disappeared on the home field side into the forever darkness of farm fields. To the east stood more corn rows behind the single scoreboard. To the west, the school bricks captured whatever light reflected off the car tops in the parking lot. And to the northwest, ever present and ever vigilant, the silhouette of St. Mary's Church silently stood watch over her football playing altar boys as they pursued small-town glory.

Carson's 26-member team came out of their locker room for the pregame warm-up. They had to cross over the school gravel parking lot between the gym and the gridiron. As they ran over the lot, the long nylon spikes in their cleats stirred the gravel and it made a rhythmic crunching noise that grew louder as they neared the field. The team's golden helmets shimmered from the reflected the lights above the field. The team snaked their way through the shadows, parked cars, and the four homecoming floats lined up to go onto the field at halftime. When the Eagles team reached the grass of the home field at the east end zone in their dark blue and gold home jerseys and white pants, the cheering from the home crowd was loud and sustained.

Noodles Cadwell's team smartly lined up on each yard line starting at the 40 to the end zone and began stretching and loosening up. Co-Captains Mark Monoly and Doug Kennedy led the team in calisthenics, while Coach Cadwell walked each yard line, stopping to say a few words to each one of his players. Noodles put his face right onto each player's facemask, going straight eye to eye, one-to-one. He confidently said the same thing to every player as he moved through the lines, "Everybody in Hubbardston, Crystal, and Carson has come here tonight to see you slay Goliath", it wasn't his usual style, but it was effective.

Sparta's team with over 75 players looked intimidating coming out on the field from the visitor's locker room. They sprinted along, crunching the gravel in the parking lot as they passed the hundreds of parked cars to get onto the other side of the field. The Spartans wore deep red and bright white uniforms with red helmets. They had 3 times as many players as did Carson. They entered this match with their state record 55 game winning streak at stake and an eye on a state championship. Unimpressed with their opponent, Sparta entered the game confident and sharp. In their pre-game drills, they looked impressive. It was a full-on contrast of teams, the number of players, each team's football history, the Spartans with total confidence, Carson City with a dream.

After calisthenics and warm-ups, each team ran a few practice offense vs defense plays on their respective sides of the field before breaking off and heading back to their respective locker rooms. In the Carson locker room, everybody sat on the floor or on the benches in front of the lockers as dads and moms, teachers, and an assortment of well-wishers passed in and out. Each gave their son or favorite boy a nod of the head, a thumbs up, or a whispered word of encouragement.

Just before it was time to play the game, Coach Noodles Cadwell entered the locker room door and sauntered to the center of the room. He motioned his team to stand and come in close. The 26 players rose and surrounded him as the well-wishers stepped back.

"Men", he said in a firm voice, as he looked around at each of the players as they crowded in as close to him as possible without touching him, "You've worked hard for so long. Tonight is your reward. It's simple now. I promise you this. Tonight you will become a champion if you hit hard, hustle on every play and execute, execute, execute!"

He raised his voice to the greatest emotion he could muster and boomed out the team's slogan, "Remember this one thing, if they don't score, we don't lose!" The team exploded in shouts of approval. Every player started slapping each other on the helmets, on the shoulder pads, and giving each other low fives and tens.

Noodles held up his hand, stared down at the floor, and the team grew quiet again. He lowered his voice and said, "Men, it's time to take off your hats and say a silent prayer. I ask that you not pray for victory, but pray to do your best. Pray to spare everyone in this game from injury." There wasn't a sound in the locker room as everyone bowed their heads.

After a moment Noodles broke the silence with an uncharacteristically soft voice, "I've asked a special guest here tonight to say a pregame prayer, Father?" From the shadows near the door, Father O'Brien appeared. No one noticed him before his introduction. It was the first time he'd visited the locker room. Father squeezed into the center of the circle of players. The priest rotated in a tight circle in the middle of the team. Father made the sign of the cross over each of us saying, "May God bless each of you boys tonight, may He keep you safe."

Coach Noodles Cadwell thanked Father and stepped into the center of the locker room. Father stepped back into the shadows near the door. The old Pennsylvania coach, tears welling in his eyes, told the team in a firm, confident voice, "Let's go tuck it to em." The boys put on their helmets. Fully stoked, every player pushed their way to the locker-room door with thumping hearts and wild screams. Spikes clattered on the tile floor; players slammed lockers. Teammates aggressively slapped on each other's shoulder pads, the sharp noise echoing off the brick walls.

The team showed up to play the big opponent. They had the confidence to win the biggest championship game of their lives. The team ran out onto that homecoming field in front of their families and friends, everyone they've ever known, everyone dreaming the same small-town dream. The teams' goal was near realization. As the moment came to them, they got the most extraordinary emotional high of their lives. It was the unique experience of being one of the unforgettable stars on a small-town undefeated and unscored upon football team.

The steel door of the locker room banged open and the team ran out straight into a surprise. For the first time, Carson's home crowd made a human pathway from the locker room to the playing field. The double line snaked through the gravel parking lot. Hundreds of people stood shoulder to shoulder, pressing in to touch the players from the locker room, across the field, and all the way to the fifty-yard line. The team ran to the field surrounded by aunts, uncles, neighbors, friends, moms, dads, classmates, teachers, doctors, nurses, farmers, clergy, businessmen, housewives, eleven Dominican nuns and a Priest, two cops, and the volunteer fire department. Everyone was yelling each player's name, screaming, ringing cowbells, and applauding wildly.

This team of twenty-six nobodies from nowhere came out to their home field. Sky-high in a fever of emotions, their self-assurance buoyed everyone. In each players' heart of hearts their success, unity, and hard work had made them certain they would beat mighty Sparta, or Michigan State, or the University of Michigan, or the Detroit Lions, or the Green Bay Packers. Completely pumped up, Carson's team projected full confidence. They exhaled an air of invincibility. The boys ran past everyone they ever knew. Every heart in the fired-up community came to will them to win.

Sparta's big man, Dwight Lowery, walked on the field ready to play. Before the season started the star running back and middle linebacker accepted a scholarship to play Big Ten Football at Michigan State University. Big and fast, Lowery led the State of Michigan in touchdowns scored. We knew him to be as tough as ten-penny nails on both sides of the ball.

Noodles drilled the team in practice the week before the title game with a special defensive strategy. He planned to make Lowery run to the inside and not let him get around the corners. He wanted to negate Lowery's impressive speed by keeping him running inside where the advantage would be to Carson's. Sparta's huge offensive line averaged 210 pounds outweighing Carson's defensive linemen by an average 35 pounds per player. Carson's team comprised speed and burning desire. The offensive line averaged only 175 lbs. But four of the five linemen ran track and could run the 100-yard dash within 1.5 seconds of the school record. Noodles

Cadwell knew he could take advantage of Sparta's over-matching size by using Carson's team speed and quickness.

To maximize the team's quickness, Noodles came up with a unique strategy to reduce penalties for being off-sides on the offensive line. The Eagles hiked the ball on the first count on every offensive play. Carson could beat every team off the ball and hit them first, a great edge in a football linemen's world.

Every coach needs to motivate their team. Noodles's motivation strategy was offbeat. He'd say something funny about the team or any of his players to motivate them and keep them loose. One of his favorites he'd tell the team with a big grin, "Boy's, my strategy of hiking the ball on the first count is necessary because I've got too many guys on this team that can't count past one," He'd get the team howling in laughter when he'd make that claim. Funny as he made it sound, it worked in every game to perfection. Noodle's strategy lured Carson's opponents into the tempo of our always hiking the ball on the one count. Several times in a game, Carson's quarterback called the famous "no play." The team came out of the huddle and headed to the line of scrimmage with no play called, instead, each player focused on being "frozen" while the quarterback barked out "Hike!" Without fail, in every game, it drew the opposing defense to jump off-sides. The result for jumping offside and hitting Carson's static offensive line was a 5-yard penalty. The resulting penalty gave Cinderella Carson City easy five-yard gains, the play almost always called with less than 5 yards to gain for a first down. It never failed.

Being the cocky un-scored upon team that Carson became over the course of the season, the Eagles made the unusual choice to always kick off the ball and go on defense to start every game. If Carson lost the coin toss to start a game, the opponents always wanted to receive, if Carson won the toss, Noodles held firm and he instructed the captains to kick-off. The Coach knew he had a great once-in-a-lifetime defense that would stop any team's offense stone-cold. He knew his defenders could be more aggressive than an offensive player to start a game, knowing that timing is more of an issue on the offense. The Coach sold the team the advantage of going on defense first. Since most of the Carson players played both on the defense and offense teams, he reasoned that by the time Carson got the ball on offense, most of the nerves present at the start of the game disappeared and his team was be ready to get down to business.

Mark and Doug came back from the start of the Sparta game coin toss ceremony. For the first and only time that season, Mark called the whole team together a few steps onto the field. He said he wanted to say something.

The team surrounded him in a circle and grew quiet as he took a place in the center of the circle of players and began speaking, his face full of emotion, "I look around at each of you and see the sons of autoworkers, the sons of farmers, sons of shopkeepers. That's what we'll be too. Soon we'll be nobodies that work on the line, in the fields, or wait on customers. The chances are, after we graduate, some of us they'll send to Vietnam. Maybe never to come back.

Tonight is our last game together. We've overcome so much to give ourselves a chance to be somebody, to be special, to do something great for which everyone will always remember each one of us. These Sparta punks think tonights game will be just another game for them. I say no. Winning has come too easy for them. But we've scratched and clawed down to our souls to get to this game. This is our time, our day, our game. I'd rather die than let Sparta win."

It was a message that resonated with each one of the Carson players, each player knew that this football game would define them in Carson for the rest of their lives. Everyone reached into the center of the circle and joined hands. Mark slapped everyone's shoulder as they reached in and on his cue, the team broke for the kickoff yelling altogether in one voice "One, Two, Three, WIN!" Nock's, in his best holler-guy voice yelled, "Time to spur this pony."

Mark took his place in the middle of the kickoff team, right next to the kicker. His job was to hustle down the field as fast as he could, blowing through every blocker on the receiving team that would watch him more than any other player on the kickoff team.

Sparta's receiving team's priority was to block Mark since from his position right next to the kicker in the center of the field, they positioned him to be the first defender to make his way down the field to tackle the kickoff receiver. In this position he'd rarely make it to the ball carrier, he'd draw blockers and typically ended up in a scrum pile while other teammates made the tackle.

Carson's band played, the crowd surrounding the field roared to life for the opening kickoff. The ball flew downfield high in the crisp autumn air, end over end. Mark chased after it. At the 40-yard line, the first of the three waves of Sparta blockers waited. One crossed around Mark's side and knocked him onto the dewy grass, but the force was only a glancing blow. Mark spun quickly to his feet. The other two lines of blockers missed his advance across the field, so the only player in Mark's view was Dwight Lowry, ball cradled in his arm, coming full force at Mark.


Lowery was alone in the middle of the field without any blockers protecting him. Mark could see his dark eyes darting left and right for an escape before realizing he had nowhere to go as Mark streaked towards him. Mark's legs pumped the ground and he flew in the Michigan night faster than he ever ran. His feet pounded the ground quicker than his heartbeat, the crisp October air was rocket fuel for his lungs bursting in and out. The noise of his feet, his heartbeat, and his intense breathing was the only sound in he could hear.

Both players put their heads down and charged at each other like angry bulls. The split second for either to back off flashed past in a nano second. Mark held his arms out and launched his body at Lowery. With a fearless heart, Mark flung himself forward at a perfect 45-degree angle to the ground.

It is a furious explosion when he hit Lowery in the midsection. The crashing noise shook the earth. White hot electricity shot through Mark's body to his every extremity. The ferocious hit created a concussion that blasted the air out of Lowery's lungs. Mark said later that the last thing he heard was Lowery's painfully loud "Rumph" that pierced the brisk night air.

The moment froze. A few hundred yards away, at the edge of the light where the darkness peers in, the black silhouette of St. Mary's Church towered over all. It was if she protected Mark, her diligent altar boy as he laid motionless, his face down in the shimmering October grass."

## Chapter 11 *The Big Game*

"How bad did Mark get hurt?", Molly asks as we rumble along, as we enter Montcalm County, our destination. "He got what we used to call a stinger," I reply. "He told us later what it was like."

Laying on the field, Mark slowly opened his eyes. The sweet smell of the cold damp fall grass from the football field started drawing him back from the silent darkness of his unconsciousness. The ground was spinning. When he lifted his head up, the glare from the lights pierced his jig-saw puzzled brain. Jumbled thoughts rattled around inside his mixed-up throbbing head. As his ears reconnected to his brain, he heard the joyful screaming Carson fans flooding into his ears. The spinning stopped and his eyes squinted past the glare. The end zone came into focus. In the background darkness he could see St. Mary's Church. Before her in the end zone, ten of his teammates grouped together and were jumping up and down, crashing into each other, ecstatically celebrating their "scoop and score" of Lowery's fumble. Mark's spectacular textbook open field tackle on Lowrey turned the game to Carson's advantage.

Mark dragged himself up to his knees, almost falling back to the ground in another rush of unconscious. With a second try, he rose to his feet and looked down at Lowrey. The Sparta Star struggled to catch a steady breath and the medical staff ran onto the field to his aid. It took Mark a moment to realize he'd knocked the wind and the football out of Lowery. His great kickoff tackle is for the ages.

He stood over Lowery and thrust both fists in the air as the Carson crowd roared their approval. He stood there, like a victorious boxer stands over his prostrated foe, as Sparta's trainers and coaches worked to help Lowery to his feet.

A few minutes passed and Carson kicked off again. Lowery, not yet recovered, stayed on the sideline while his substitute knelt in the end zone with the ball, signaling a touch back. The sub saw Mark roaring down the field straight at him and took the cowards knee to avoid getting hit. The referees moved the ball to the 20-yard line and Lowery came back into the game once more for Sparta's first offensive play.

Lowery came back into the game. He got the ball on their first play. He ran around the Carson end and headed up the field. It looked like a long gain. But Mark came out of nowhere. He hit him violently from the side. Mark was the left side outside linebacker and had come hustling across the field with his 185-pound body running at full speed. The sound of his hitting Lowery rattled across the field and he drilled Lowery about 10 yards out of bounds, through the sideline ropes behind the bench, and into the second row of the Sparta fans' bleachers. Mark's second big hit stunned Lowery. He struggled to pull himself up to his feet as the Sparta fans gasped at the ferocious hit. The site of the hard hit on their star player hushed them to silence. Across the field, Carson's crowd went wild. Mark popped up to his feet at the sideline and just pointed his index finger at Lowery. The game was as good as over right then.

Sparta punted the ball one down later and that was as close as the game ever got as The Carson City-Crystal Area Eagles won their first homecoming since what we thought was the dawn of recorded time by a score of 28-0. Mark Monoly played out of his mind that night. He seemed to know exactly when Lowery was to get the ball and on almost every play Mark burst through would-be blockers and hit Lowery harder than a speeding freight train. Mark recorded a school record 24 tackles in the game. Lowery had the worst game of his stellar career, carrying the football 23 times for a minus 14 yards rushing.

Late in the game, the Carson City Eagles had the ball and drove down to the 20-yard line. They led Sparta with an insurmountable 21-0 lead. With only 20 seconds left on the game clock, Mark walked over to the referee and called a surprising time out. He came to the huddle saying, "Guys, Nocks has practiced against us every day, he takes lots of punishment. He took a lot of beatings, but he never backed down from any of us. Nocks never gets much game time. Let's pull him off the bench and let him score a touchdown!"

Every tired, dirty, grass-stained lineman looked up to Mark in the huddle and said "yeah, let's do it." Carson's running back Tim Fitzgerald said, "Fellas, I'm hurt" and he limped towards the sidelines in obvious faked pain. Noodles Cadwell looked puzzled and came out on the field to meet Tim. Tim whispered to the Coach what was going on.  Noodles nodded and smiled, then motioned for Nocks, waving him into the game.

Out from the small pack of players lining the sideline, most of whom were all grass stained and dirty, The Nocks, our beloved holler guy, came running out to get instructions from Noodles.  His uniform sparkling clean, Nocks strapped on his caged helmet and he came trotting onto the field.  The team waved and cheered Nocks on as he came to the huddle. "Nocks," Mark said, "you are going into the tailback slot."  Nocks looked shocked.  He never played the running back position before, even in practice.

Everyone in the huddle, tired as they were, perked up for one last touchdown, this one for the Nocks.  Mark, the best blocker on the team, switched places with the fullback and said, "Nocks, just follow me."

Carson's offensive team found a fresh source of energy. The most popular and least talented player on the team came into the game to cap the magical season.  In unison, the team yelled, "1,2,3 break." The team broke the huddle and sprinted up to the line.  Waiting for them was the tired, shocked, and all but beaten Sparta team who grudgingly took their defensive positions.  Quarterback David O'Shea called out the signals "Ready set, hike."  Carson's center hiked the ball and David spun around and handed the ball off to Nocks. He ran behind Mark Monoly, straight up the middle.

The Eagles fired up offensive linemen created a gigantic hole in Sparta's now demoralized and tired defensive line. Square in the middle of the gap and ready to tackle Nocks was Sparta's all-star middle linebacker Dwight Lowery. Mark saw Lowery and revved up to full speed, lowered his shoulders, and drove his face mask right between the numbers on Lowery's jersey. Mark hit him full of fire and kept his feet pumping, driving Lowery backwards with all his might.

Nocks cradled the football tightly in is arms and ran right behind Mark. With his shoulders down, he ran with his chest pressed right on Mark's back. Mark kept his balance and kept driving Lowery as the crowd erupted one last time. Lowery seemed to stop his backward momentum for an instant, but Mark bore down hard with one last huge push.

Lowery took the hit and tumbled backwards into the end zone. As Nocks and Mark crashed forward, Mark looked up and saw the old wooden white goal posts twisting and falling to the ground as players from both teams scattered out of the way. Mark had driven Dwight Lowery through the left leg of the goal posts and they crashed to the ground. The referees signaled a touchdown and sounded the final gun to end the game. All the Carson players rushed to Nocks and hoisted him jubilantly on their shoulders while the Sparta players walked slowly off the field, their collective heads hanging low in disbelief. Sparta's long winning streak ended in, of all the improbable places, Carson City.

The hometown fans swamped the field. Estatic Carson players on the sideline danced and laughed and held their helmets high in the air as they ran out to the end zone. They carried the dazed and bespectacled Nocks on their shoulders, his uniform still sparkling clean, in the pandemonium created by the game ending touchdown. Nocks, even though he'd never played running back, let alone ever dreamed he'd get into a game, or even thought about scoring a touchdown, was beaming brighter than the field lights. The elation of this win overcame every member of the Eagle team. The celebration felt better knowing they were sharing a glorious moment with the team's least capable player, but a guy who gave his all, on every play each day in practice.

There was absolute mayhem in the locker room after the game, Coach Noodles couldn't even keep his tough guy persona going in his post-game chat. He talked about how the team's hard work paid off, but he couldn't keep it together. His voice broke when he said he'd never coached a better team. He broke down in tears saying "I love you guys" before the team grabbed him and, fully clothed, carried him into the showers. Anybody who came into that locker room that night received the same free shower, including Father O'Brien, who went home all smiles and grinning in his wet clothes, Roman collar and all.

After the game, the homecoming dance started in the high school cafetorium. Because it was homecoming, a live disk jockey from WION in Ionia was on stage. The cafetorium lights were dim and the whole high school waited for the football players to come in from the locker room. The team arrived in small groups. As they entered the cafetorium, the room erupted in screams and cheers. The team members were wearing their royal blue and gold varsity jackets. A few had limps. Others sported band aids on their hands or faces. But every player returned the enthusiastic welcome with hands raised high over their heads. They flashed beaming smiles to acknowledge their newfound status of being a champion.

After the dance, Mark and a couple of carloads of giddy players found their way over to the parent's party at Max Boyle's house. Mr. Boyle was the shop teacher at the school and tonight it was his turn to host more than a party. He held an ecstatic community celebration.

Max spent his summer breaks from teaching doing carpentry side jobs for the school and local citizens who contracted his services. His loud, deep booming voice didn't seem to fit his short 5-foot 5-inch body. When Max spoke, he did so with unquestioned confidence. But his carpentry skills didn't match his confidence. His many projects were so poorly done that everyone called him by the moniker "Max the Axe." No one ever earned a more fitting nickname.

Max the Axe loved the players. He never missed a Carson City football game and he came to most of the team's practices. He was ready with an opinion on any subject under the sun, but his favorite topic was the play of the football team. Max held an old school philosophy. He'd say to get the best out of the players, the coaches needed "to kick them hard to get them to play hard." Max the Axe loved to criticize the players. But he had a lovable nature about him. Every player knew his sharp barbs were meant to motivate the team. Only Max could blast a stream of denunciations like he did and not offend anyone. When he needled a football player, it felt more like a compliment.

Everyone on the team loved it when Max the Axe called them out with a verbal hazing. No player escaped being torched with a Max the Axism. In one game Tim Fitzgerald scored an amazing four touchdowns and rushed for 250 yards, but all Max could talk about was Tim having fumbled the ball late in that Carson blowout victory.

In a game earlier in the season Mark made 15 tackles, an excellent game by anyone's measure. But hawk-eyed Max spotted the single instance in the game when a big lineman got the best of Mark. At every opportunity Max would roll his sparkling eyes and whine to Mark saying, "Monoly, I'm so embarrassed for your poor dad. He stood there on the sidelines of the Pewamo-Westphalia game and watched you getting your ass kicked by that fat German kid." Mark couldn't even mount a defense. He just shook his head and had grinned.

The team's favorite "Max the Axe" story was when Max, always the home announcer at football games, caused the team to shake their heads in humorous disbelief out on the field one night. The opposing team ran the Statue of Liberty, a throw back play from the early days of football. The opposing team's quarterback dropped back, held the ball out as if to pass, when a running back came around behind him, grabbed the ball, and ran for a big gain.

After that play Carson's defensive team went into their huddle and as they were planning the next play, Max's booming voice came over the field from the press box, amplified by the public address loudspeakers. "Well folks, that was the Statue of Liberty play, the oldest play in football, and it just fooled every player on Carson's team."  All the players in Carson's huddle heard that comment, the entire team started belly laughing and couldn't stop. Carson had to call a timeout to regain their composure.  Mark added to the levity Max's comment caused, "Geeze, we don't even have a home field advantage with Max the Axe working us over from the booth."

Finding out where the parents were partying after the football games and crashing it had become a little game for the team during the season. The team couldn't wait to invade Max's season ending party. After the homecoming dance, Mark and the rest of the team got in their cars and drove to the Boyle's.

In the dark outside Max Boyle's house they pounded on the doors, windows, and side of the house, chanting in unison for food.  Max opened the front door and yelled "You guys get off my property!  It's past your curfew. Go home!' But the players all poured right past him and rushed into the house. The parents, faculty, and well-wishing friends and neighbors greeted them with applause, cheers, and lots of hugs. Max feigned displeasure at the intrusion, but he was glad the players came to his house.

The adults had been celebrating extra that night and everyone was pretty well loaded up on booze, including Noodles. Mark teased him and shouted over the din. "Coach how about a victory beer for me and the boys?" Noodles, holding a long neck Strohs in his hand laughed and said "You guys deserve a beer, you can have all the root beer you can hold!" and the team all booed him as he laughed and put his arm around Mark, raising his brown bottle of beer up above his head.

The team disposed of any food left about the house while the boys and Noodles regaled the party with stories of plays made during the game. Mark, while unsuccessfully attempting to grab Noodle's beer, shouted out over the party din "It was a brilliant game played by superior athletes overcoming timid coaching" to the laughter of the partygoers. Noodles responded teasing back, "Every parent here knows what a challenge this group is. Great parents made it happen. A bit of coaching got us over the top. We've all seen this group's shaky grades. This season was a miracle!"

Nocks was still clinging to the football he'd carried

across the goal line for the final touchdown of the game. The Nocks was in fine form. "Hey Coach, did you see the shifty footwork and change of direction I made to score that touchdown?  I must have broken five tackles on that brilliant run. These Larry Cadodee offensive linemen forgot how to block so I had to do my moves," he said as he danced and did spins as everyone laughed at the slowest guy on the team, our version of a ruptured elephant, now playfully embellishing his moment of glory.

Max yelled incredulously at Nocks, "I suppose now Gusnocki you think you should have been our starting tailback for the season?" which spawned howls of amusement and catcalls from everyone in the room. Nocks, always ready to top any challengers, replied. "Heck no, I should have been the starting quarterback," and with that remark he won the room. Everyone roared their approval.  He finally gave up the football, tossing it around the room to the players and coaches, asking everyone on the team to sign it for him as a keepsake. It was great. It was always great fun to crash the after-game parties but when the Max the Axe ran out of food, the players got into their cars and headed on down to their last stop, The American Legion club.

The team blew open the Legion Club doors.  The patron's enthusiastic response greeted them, everyone there started yelling and clapping as the team came in the door.  As Mark entered the building, he thought he might not be welcome.  It surprised him when the Legionnaires gave him a little extra applause when he entered the bar. Parents and anyone left off the Max the Axe party invite list gathered at the Legion Club after the game to celebrate the big win and the perfect season.

The players found their parents to fleece them for snacks. Better yet, cash. The rest of the team was mingling with the crowd or brashly bellying up to the bar where they took advantage of all the distractions in the club to beg bartender and rabid football fan Smoke Burke for celebratory beers. He snuck more than a few cold brewskys over the bar to the underage victors.

Everybody wanted to see the local TV report of the night's high school football scores. Before the sports came on, the lead story was about the national anti-Vietnam War demonstration in Washington DC. The room full of veterans grew quiet as they listened to the reports about the protest. They described it as the largest demonstration in the country's history. Like everywhere in America, there was a growing disagreement among the club members about the war. But without exception, the Legionnaires supported the troops. The vets who still supported the war shouted their disgust with the protesters who got air time by burning flags and draft cards.

Moms in the club gave a worried glance at their joyful sons. Half of them turned 18 that autumn and registered for the draft, the rest of boys soon to follow.

The war had dragged on so long that there was no end in sight, despite the promises of President Nixon. His re-election campaign promised that there was a light at the end of the tunnel. The news report divided room in an uneasy quiet between supporters of the war and those there who were anti-war.

Carson's win over Sparta led the sports report and the bar exploded in cheers at the announcement. Everyone jumped to their feet and started cheering when the reporter said, "Cinderella Carson City is wearing glass slippers tonight. They turned in a perfect season, the Eagles pulling off one of the greatest upsets in Michigan high school football history." The reporter exclaimed, "We never thought we'd put these words in the same sentence, but tonight we can. "Carson City"; "Undefeated"; "Unscored upon"; "Perfect Season." It was amazing to hear our school name on TV and to hear our coach's name too.

They mentioned several of our players for their contribution, including star player Wendel Brooks. Wendel's mention made the night even more fun. No one on the team had the name of either Wendel or Brooks. Wendel's accolades didn't ruin the night, the party continued and years later people ask about whatever happened to Wendel Brooks.

Mark's pregame prediction was spot on for most of us, playing on this football team was the pinnacle of our lives, the night was one to remember and savor forever, a night of pure joy. Players continued hustling parents for burgers until the wee hours when

Smoke closed the night out announcing "Last call" to a loud chorus of boos from the jam-packed Legion Club.

## Chapter 12 *The Aftermath*

"So, my Dad played championship football eh?" Molly said with a little less of a mocking tone in her voice as we continued our journey eastward past small towns, farms, and the spattering of Michigan woodlands. "Are you joking me, you on an undefeated football team?"

"Yes," I reply "And don't forget, we were unscored upon too. It's known as a perfect season." I add now the dad lesson. "Being part of that team's experience changed us for the better. Kids fortunate to play on excellent football teams have exceptional, character building experiences. But we had many obstacles. When I look back on it now, I realize how really special it was." Then I add, "It's a lengthy story if you want to hear it, but it wasn't long after the season when we had the worst experience of our lives." Molly, I knew, was too curious in her DNA to not want to know the full story and she quickly bites, "What happened Dad?" she asks.

I can see she's fully engaged and I begin. "It started the week after our championship winning football game against Sparta on that Friday night. The community was still in the highest of spirits from the perfect football season. Not ready to let the marvelous feelings go by so soon, the high school administration approved a "Championship Dance" request from Brenna Brennan and Darby Donahue.

Mark had approached the 2 girls about leading a committee to put together the special dance to celebrate the success of the team. Brenna got her dad to cover the costs, Darby got her parents to solicit the local merchants to make in-kind donations. They worked hard and the dance was at the usual place, the high school cafetorium. The girls hired a live band, something very rare for our small school, from somewhere out of town. They organized parents to bring in tons of food and they organized the committee to deck the school cafetorium out in blue and gold decorations."

The night of the dance, they had the cheerleaders in full battle dress and pom-poms. The cheerleaders lined up near the front door of the cafetorium and every time a team member arrived and meandered into the cafetorium, they greeted them with a nice cheer, pom-poms shaking. All the kids at the dance followed their lead and gave each player a hero's welcome.

Darby and Brenna plans were on the mark and everyone enjoyed the dance. The football players got special treatment and spent the night dancing to the music, eating food, talking with the prettiest girls, reveling in their football heroics. Like all school dances, this one had plenty of chaperons, about a dozen, half were teachers and the other half volunteer parents.

One reluctant chaperone was Reverend Horace Clark, the school board member from the Butternut Reformed Church. He normally wouldn't go to a sinful dance but, because there was an agreement in the school board charter that the board would have at least one-member present for school functions, his name was in the rotation and he pulled the duty. He sure wasn't there to dance; his church forbade such activity.

Mr. Petterson was also a chaperone at the dance. The standard teacher's contract required him to do three chaperoning events per year, but with typical new teacher enthusiasm, he volunteered past his contract obligations because Brenna and Darby had reached out to him. They were two of his favorite students. He also knew a first-year, non-seniority teacher like himself doing extra duties helped make a favorable impression on the administration. Petterson saw this small town come to life during the football season. Being asked to chaperone the dance made him happy. He thought it to be easy and fun to do.

Mr. Petterson didn't know or expect to see his nemesis from the school board, Mr. Clark, at the dance. When he first saw Clark in the cafetorium, he tried to avoid the Reverend as best he could. But soon Horace Clark spotted Petterson and approached him. Clark started engaging Mr. Peterson in the ongoing battle of what Clark had labeled "A lack of decency and Christian morals" he claimed was emanating from Petterson's English department and bubbled over like poison into the student body.

The day Clark criticized Petterson in an open school board meeting for approving and assigning the novel "Henderson the Rain King," it was easy to see the Fundamentalist Baptist Minister/Gas Station

Proprietor was gunning for the young liberal from Minnesota.

Soon the two men were in an animated discussion near the edge of the dance floor and students began gathering about to listen in. Clark said that Mark's behaviors in the Sparta football game annoyed him. He described it as embarrassingly poor sportsmanship. Clark brought up Mark's protesting of the Vietnam War at Boys State while he was a guest of the American Legion describing it as "near treason."
Petterson irritated Clark by defending Monoly's protest of the Vietnam War, saying it was a perfect example of a citizen's right of free speech. That assertion got Clark more animated. He stepped closer to Mr. Petterson, aggressively leaning his 6 ft. 4-inch frame over the diminutive Petterson. Clark's deep booming voice grew increasingly more hostile.

Darby and Brenna were the first of many students to notice the confrontation. "Oh no," Brenna said to Darby. "We need to get Mr. Petterson away from Reverend Clark before they ruin the dance." Darby and Brenna were not in Reverend Clarks' line of vision, they were standing behind him feverishly motioning to Mr. Petterson to break off the debate and come with them.

"Petterson, you're a troublemaker, we didn't have all this moral decay in school until you came along with your dirty books" Clark said, his cheeks beet red in anger and his voice rising above the din of music bouncing off the cement block walls and shiny grey

194

linoleum floor in the half-darkened cafetorium. Petterson, seeing Darby and Brenna motioning to him, started to excuse himself but changed his mind when Clark blamed him for what Clark was claiming to be Petterson's negative impact on students. He stood his ground and was quick to rejoin Clark saying in a calm, respectful, but loud voice that "Good literature is the fundamental right of every citizen Mr. Clark. It enriches our lives, gives us wisdom to be, to think. These kids deserve the freedom of thought and expression. They need to learn so they can think, problem solve, live exemplary lives. That's not stirring up trouble, that's rejecting ignorance." That remark set Clark off, "Are you calling me ignorant?" Clark shouted.

Darby hated Reverend Clark and with that remark from him, she couldn't hold it back any longer. She shouted in a cutting voice that "Ignorant is beyond your capabilities Horace, you're just a big dumb ass farmer with a big mouth." Clark's face got redder and he whirled around and pointed his finger at poor Brenna, mistakenly thinking Brenna had made the disparaging remark. He yelled over his shoulder at Petterson while pointing at Brenna, "Do you see the trash you're encouraging?"

Brenna couldn't handle the hostility. No one had ever verbally abused her before. She never said anything confrontational, she was a model of respectful manners. Brenna always gave full respect to everyone, her parents always the perfect example of how to treat everyone well. She exuded tenderness and fragility, and Reverend Clark's yelling at her in such a crude way cut her to the bone. In an instant she was weeping and sobbing. Darby put her arms protectively around Brenna and looked up at Clark and screamed at him again. "Why are you picking on Brenna, she didn't do anything!"

At the instant Brenna started crying, Mark joined the growing circle around the two men. The first thing he heard was Clark's disparaging remark about Brenna. He saw Brenna sobbing and pushed his way to the inner circle. A scuffle started, not between Petterson and Clark, but between the Reverend Clark and Mark. No one who was there could say with certainty if Clark or Mark started the physical confrontation.

Mark later explained that he stepped in to defend Brenna from the verbal insults of Clark. Clark ended up on the floor. In the fall, he broke his right arm, and a flurry of activity started like a line of dominoes falling. One of the parent chaperons called the local telephone operator. The operator, trained to handle emergencies in these pre-911 days, called for an ambulance. Deputy Barney Fife, the sole officer on patrol that night, heard the ambulance's siren and followed it up to the school.

Carson's Police Chief Glenn Hughes was taking the week after homecoming off for some upper peninsula deer hunting with a few of the local city council members and left town putting Barney in charge. After the fact, everyone in town said if Glenn were there that night, he'd have handled the whole ugly incident better.

Glenn's solid judgment and people skills were the main small-town weapons he used in keeping most fracases off the record. Glenn used common sense in these kinds of encounters, he knew from his experience of policing in a village where everyone knew everyone else that any adjudication could live a long life in infamy.

But Barney Fife was young and ambitious. When the ambulance took Clark to the hospital, Glenn was not there to impart his wisdom to the inexperienced deputy. Barney saw a chance to make a rare arrest on his own initiative. Making arrests is rare in small towns. Making one could be a career enhancing event for a young deputy looking to make a name for himself.

After arriving at the school Barney Fife arrested Mark. He read him his rights and put him into the back of the police car, charging him with assault and battery.
    It was a dark seminal moment that changed the trajectory of Mark's life.

Because Mark was 18 years old, they arraigned him the following Monday morning in Montcalm County Circuit Court. The judge was Dwight Lowery Sr., the father of the star Sparta running back that Mark had single handily destroyed two weeks earlier in the championship football game. Mark brought his parents and his lawyer to the hearing. When the proceedings started the assistant prosecutor read the charges. The prosecutor asserted Mark had, with malice and intent, assaulted Reverend Horace Clark and had broken his arm. The prosecution claimed they had a list of witnesses who saw the attack.

Instead of asking for a plea from the defense, Judge Lowery called for a brief recess. He instructed all parties to meet in his chambers.

Lowery sat in his high-backed leather chair behind his desk and said, "Please everyone, take a seat." The prosecutor, Mark's parents, Mark, and his attorney brought chairs up around the judge's desk in a semi-circle for everyone.


"Mr. Monoly," Judge Lowery said to Mark, "I recall seeing you play football a few weeks ago and I see that you are an outstanding athlete. But I noted your display of poor sportsmanship. Being out of control and doing that taunting, it doesn't surprise me you find yourself here with some very serious charges against you. The prosecutor tells me this is an open-and-closed case. I will tell you these are very serious charges and the injuries you've caused to Reverend Clark will require, under Michigan law, a jail sentence if we convict you. You are looking at 5-10 years in the Ionia State Petitionary. You are a youthful man, barely legal at 18 years old. Your life will be permanently and forever affected by a felony conviction and incarceration.


I think the State and all concerned think there may be a better solution to this, so I propose, if the prosecution agrees, that we regroup in one hour. I would encourage the prosecutor to drop these charges if you arrive back in my court one hour hence with proof that you have joined the United States Army." Judge Lowery made a glance to the prosecutor, and as if choreographed, the prosecutor nodded her head in agreement."

Judge Lowery continued. "Volunteering for the draft is the fastest way to get into the service. You can do that at the recruiting office, it's easy to find, just one block west of the courthouse. I've directed my court clerk to call ahead and the folks there are waiting for your arrival, Mr. Monoly. I believe that service to your country in its time of need would be the best solution for everyone involved in this incident. In the Army you can pursue your high school diploma, further your education, or develop job skills. The court believes that some discipline and regimen will help you get your personal issues straightened out. I'm confident in a couple of years when you return to civilian life, you'll be an exemplary citizen. Prison, if that is your choice, will afford you no such opportunities."

Mark's mother was weeping into Mark's dad's shoulder. Mark's face drained as he nodded meekly in agreement. He knew there wasn't an actual choice here.

When the court came back from the one-hour adjournment, Mark came into the courtroom with his enlistment paperwork for Judge Lowery to inspect.

"Madam Prosecutor" Lowery began, "This court can confirm Mr. Monoly is a patriot and has enlisted himself in the armed forces of the United States of America." "I recommend that these charges against him be waived and we not stand in his way of coming to the defense of our country. What do you say?" The prosecutor said, "The State agrees to drop all charges in lieu of the enlistment of Mr. Monoly into the service of our country." And with that, Mark Monoly, a typical innocent high school boy from rural America, was on his way to Vietnam."

The following Thursday night, the Carson City Crystal Area School board held its regular meeting. The opening topic concerned the details of how Horace Clark's arm got broken. Several witnesses on both sides gave conflicting accounts of who did what in the incident. The school board failed to pass a motion to reprimand both Petterson and Clark for the brouhaha. Instead, they inserted into the official minutes a statement declaring Mark Monoly responsible for Clark's injury. The board included in the minutes a statement saying Mark's arrest caused him to join the Army as an alternative to being criminally prosecuted for assaulting Clark.

When the board approved the minutes, Horace Clark addressed the members and the large audience. "The events of last Friday night underscore the lack of respect from our student body that I have been speaking about since my election to this board. I've watched this horrible Monoly kid embarrass our community while being a sponsored guest of our American Legion Club at Boys State. There he tried leading a revolt against our country. This same scoundrel then displayed unbelievable poor sportsmanship during a high-profile football game. He brought shame upon us all when he should have made our community proud.   Now he avoids prosecution by shamelessly joining the Army after physically assaulting a community leader.

I say this to you not to criticize this lost adolescent man.  I want to hold him as an example.  He reflects the sad state of affairs ongoing this very day in the classrooms we are here to protect.   We've been elected to insure our children grow up the right way, we're here to ensure these youngsters grow to become productive, god fearing exemplary citizens.

It is clear our English department violated our moral standards.   Mr. Petterson brings obscene material into our schools.  He is corrupting the impressionable minds of our youth.   This material stirred up uncontrollable dark passions in this unfortunate childish man. The mistakes he's made are too long to count.

Mr. Petterson induced the English Department to go off to some New York source of approval for materials for our children to read.  Friends, I remind you we are not in New York City; We reject New York values; we have our own values to protect.

Tonight, I am proposing a simple solution to win back our schools from Mr. Petterson's misguided leadership.  I am making a motion that 1) requires that we, the school board, will read and approve every book assigned to our student's curriculum before teachers may assign it to students.  The same policy would apply before we stock a book in the Library and 2) pass a resolution banning "Henderson the Rain King" from our list of approved books because of its obscene content." The board, loaded with Clark's cronies, passed his motion without discussion.

# Chapter 13 *Saying Goodbye*

Molly pulled the Jeep up to the stop sign at the junction of M57 and Meyers Lake Avenue outside of Sparta. Before pulling onto the highway and turning east, she asked incredulously, "Are you saying the Judge railroaded Mark Monoly into joining the Army because he made the Judge's son look like a fool in a football game? "No one knows what was in his heart, Molly. It happened many years ago, but people in Carson still believe Judge Lowery acted in bad faith. "I can't believe the Judge did that Dad; I would have been so mad." "We were mad Molly; we were mad and more.

It wasn't uncommon back then where a young guy over the age of 18 got into a minor bit of trouble with the law. To avoid adjudication and the threat of incarceration, judges gave them an alternative to go into the military service. Recruiters for the military services were finding it hard to find volunteers, as a result they put the draft into effect. Despite the draft, the war created a military manpower shortage. The fact is the War in Vietnam was unpopular and every day the public's resistance grew against it.

Lots of Vietnam era vets are guys like Mark who had scrapes with the law. Most draftees were guys that couldn't, or didn't want to attend college. An otherwise healthy draftee could get an educational deferment by going to college and avoid being drafted altogether, at least until graduation. Because of this, there are perceptions that the Vietnam Vets comprise less educated and less affluent men when compared to other wars. Fair or not, many people say our failure in Vietnam is because we put a lower quality of soldier into the conflict.

Gladys Hooper ran our local draft board since before World War Two. Every man in the county 18 and older referred to her as Aunt Gladys. The senior boys in the class of 1970 started receiving letters from Aunt Gladys a few weeks before they turned 18 years old. The letters were notices. It required them under penalty of law to register for the draft. Everywhere else in the world the words "Wham Bam, thank you Ma'am" has a different meaning than how we knew the phrase. For draft aged men in Montcalm County, it described how fast Aunt Gladys would get a guy inducted into the service.

For Mark, everything happened so quickly he didn't even return to high school before they inducted him. Mark's forced application into the draft occurred on a Monday afternoon. The draft office had him shipping out to basic training the following Monday. Mark and the rest of us found out the rumors were true. A wham bam thank you ma'am courtesy of Aunt Gladys got a guy into the army lightning fast.

It was mid-week when Father O'Brien got the news about the enlistment and he gave Mark a call. Mark answered the phone and heard the familiar voice saying, "Mark, this is Father O'Brien. I understand that you're leaving for the service next week. Is that true?" "Yes, it is Father," Mark replied, his voice cracking with emotion.

Before Mark could say another word, Father O'Brien said, "Mark, we can talk about the details anytime you want, but I would love you to come and serve the 5 pm Saturday night Mass before you leave. It would give this old priest an opportunity to say a proper goodbye to you." "I wouldn't leave town without saying goodbye to you Father," Mark replied and continued. "If you don't mind, can I get my best friend Richard Gusnocki to serve Mass with us one last time?" Father answered, "Absolutely, there's no better choice. It will flatter Richard when you ask him."

Mark and Nocks served the Saturday 5 pm service just like they had countless times. After Mass, Father O'Brien and his two long-serving and favorite altar boys came into the vestibule. Father, as he always did, set his chalice down on the auxiliary altar and reverently bent over to kiss it before locking it away.

The priest turned around and faced Mark. Father's eyes were welling with tears, and with the compassion of the most devoted of small parish priests he said, in a soft kind voice, "Mark, since the day you first served Mass back when you were just a tyke, I could see you would be a faithful altar boy. I could see you were dependable, sincere, and possessing Faith. I'm sure Richard will agree with me when I say that you've been one of the best altar boys that ever-served Mass here." Father, his voice full of emotion, continued on saying, "Thank you Mark, for all your service these many years. I wish you the best in the next phase of your life. I promise I will keep you in my daily prayers until the day God takes me home."

The depth of feeling this wonderful priest expressed touched Mark's heart, it showed in his tear-filled eyes. Mark looked down at the floor and the only thing he could say was a mumbled "Thank you Father." Father was emotional too and cleared his throat before continuing, "Mark, kneel down and let me give you a special blessing."

Mark got down on his knees on the hard vestibule floor and Father nodded to Nocks who stood beside Mark. Nocks put his hand on his friend's shoulder. Father's voice, now back into the tone of voice of a priest in command began his blessing of Mark, "Dear Lord, we pray that you keep our son Mark safe from all harm and return him to his family and this community that loves him. He is a wonderful boy and here in Your church and in Your service, he has grown to be a good Catholic and a fine young man. I ask in Your name to forgive his sins and trespasses." Father O'Brien made the sign of the cross over Mark's head and blessed him. "In the name of the Father, Son, and Holy Spirit." Mark got up and Father reached out his hand and gave Mark a firm, warm man-to-man handshake. "I'll miss you Mark, I'd love it if you'd pay me a visit when you come home." "I will," said Mark. "Keep my cassock around and if it still fits, I'll serve Mass for you again." Father's face lit up with his trademark smile and he replied, "I'll look forward to that." With that, they parted ways.

Mark and Nocks walked back across the main altar into the altar boy sacristy to take off their cassocks and surpluses. As they hung them up in the altar boy's closet, Nocks said to Mark, "Man, we've got a surprise farewell party planned for you tonight. The gang is getting together on the State land down south of Hubbardston, we've got a keg of beer on ice and it's ready to go. Everybody's waiting for us. It will be awesome!"

Mark's eyes lit up and he said, "Everything's been moving so fast I hadn't even considered a farewell party. That's awesome Nocks." Nocks replied, "To be sure you don't go all Larry Cadodee on us, I'm taking you hostage, let's get going." "I'm in for sure," said Mark, and with that they skipped down the aisle of the now empty church and out the front door. They climbed happily into Nock's red 1967 Toyota Corolla and headed out to the farewell grasser.

Whenever the weather was warm, it was grasser season. There were lots of areas where we'd drive our dad's muscle cars of the late 1960s into a secluded wood. Grassers were a bring your own affair, but Nocks was lucky to procure a beer for everyone.


The class of 1970 was one of the last generations of middle American kids to grow up without easy access to drugs. Drugs were part of the youth culture, especially in the late 1960s music, and drugs were a central topic in the news. Every magazine and every newscast ran features about kids using LSD, uppers, downers, and marijuana. But the fact is drugs yet to reach rural towns. The vice of choice for rural high schoolers was alcohol.

Secluded openings the woods were the best spots for grassers. We'd find spots somewhere in the country with enough room to circle a couple dozen cars. With the engines off, everyone tuned in the same FM radio station and rolled down the windows of their cars so the music would surround the party goers. We'd build a small bonfire in the center of the cars and everyone would have a ready seat on the hoods. Most parents were aware we held occasional grassers. But they turned a blind eye to them because most rural kids were smart enough not to drink and drive. Every carload of partying kids nominated a driver to stay sober for the night. It kept everyone safe.

Nocks got Louie Casey to help him get the keg of beer for Mark's grasser. Louie was a kid in the senior class that looked like he was much older than his 17 years. Louie found a quiet rural liquor store about 5 miles east of Carson City. It was out of the school district in Perrington, a town of about 100, and Louie could buy booze there. At the Secretary of State's Driver's License office, Louie claimed to have lost his driver's license and ordered a duplicate for a fee of $5.00.


With a steady hand cutting out a few numbers on his duplicate license with an exacto razor knife, Louie adjusted his birth date. He instantly became a credible looking 22-year-old. When he and Nocks picked up the keg, Louie bought a few pints of Southern Comfort, the reputed favorite beverage of rocker Janis Joplin. Shots of bourbon and beer chasers were the drinks available the night of Mark's farewell grasser.

The sun had just gone down when Nocks and Mark drove into the last open spot in the circle of cars out in the boonies. Mark stepped out of the car. It surprised him to be greeted to cheers from the 60 partygoers and well-wishers ready for letting it all hang out in the woods. Nocks turned off the car and the headlights and put his car radio on the same station everyone was listening to before joining the revelry. The campfire was blazing away in the center of the circle, cold beer and Southern Comfort flowed like water. Kids sat on car hoods, some danced to the music on the radios. Everyone moved about the circle, pouring beer into styrofoam cups from the keg. The occasion for the party made the mood low key and reserved. Everyone came by Nock's Toyota to spend a few moments reminiscing with Mark. He spent his last night shaking hands and giving goodbye hugs to each of his many friends.

Darby Donahue and Brenna Brennan were the most difficult of the goodbyes. Brenna was red eyed from frequent bursts of crying throughout the evening. She spent the entire night within arm's reach of Mark, finally working up the poise to say goodbye without tearing up when she spoke to Mark. She put her arms around him and gave a long heartfelt hug while saying: "I don't know what to do when you're gone Mark, you've always been like a big brother to me. I've always felt that you were forever near, always watching over me to be sure nobody pulled any monkey business on me. When a guy got fresh and you were around, you took care of me. If a teacher was on me for not having a right answer in class, you'd whisper the answer to me. This isn't fair. That Horace Clark, he's the one that needs to go to the Army." Mark smiled wistfully and said, "Brenna, you don't need me for anything, you're the most awesome person ever. But I'll miss you too. Let's hang out when I'm back in town." Their embrace was the longest of the many goodbye hugs that night.

Darby was right behind Brenna, but the sharp tongue and wit we knew her for left her this evening. She was uncharacteristically remorseful and self-effacing. "Mark this is my fault." She began, "If I hadn't goaded that dumb Horace Clark this never would have happened. I should have just shut my big mouth and walked away." Mark responded, "Now Darby, those Dominican nuns taught us to take a stand when things aren't right. It's what we both did. We shouldn't have to feel bad about that.

It wasn't you that took it to the physical level either, that was me. That was my colossal mistake. I'm not one bit sorry for Horace Clark. He got what he deserved. But Darby, please don't blame yourself, it's not your fault. It was me that got in a fight with that big dumb cluck." Darby, who's nature had her being a little distant from people, jumped into Mark's arms for a long embrace and whispered to him, "I love you Mark, I'll miss you so much. I'll pray for you every day."

Late in the party, a set of car headlights blazed through the darkness of the woods. The lights got everyone's the attention. Underage drinkers worried about police raids that would result in a minor's in possession (MIP) charge, so everyone moved towards their cars, ready to flee the scene if it was the police. The car stopped outside the circle, the lights went out, and the unmistakable rumbling baritone voice of Max the Axe roared out, "Where's Monoly?" Max the Axe stepped out from out of the darkness and into the flickering light of the campfire in the inner circle of the cars. Right behind him was Mr. Petterson and Coach Noodles Cadwell. "I'm over here, Mr. Petterson!", Mark shouted over the music. The three men walked past small groups of incredulous teenagers towards the sound of Mark's voice, finding him sitting on the hood of Nock's Toyota surrounded by most of the senior class. The students stood there in stunned silence, everyone tensed up, wondering how the teachers found them. They nervously waited to see what was next to come.

All eyes were on the three teachers. As the men approached, everyone thought big trouble was coming to hit them. Max's loud sarcastic voice broke the silence, "Isn't this just pathetic, you losers are out here in the middle of nowhere partying it up like you don't have enough trouble. And look at you Monoly, you're supposed to be one of the smarter ones in your class but noooo, you've hit a new high in lows."

Mark shook his head and couldn't help but crack a smile. Before he could say anything Max the Axe barked out "Gusnocki where are you?" and the Nocks slowly pushed his way to the front of the gathering circle of kids. "Where's the keg, Gusnocki?" Max demanded. Nocks answered back in his most innocent sounding and insincere voice, "Uh, there's no keg here, Mr. Boyle."

"Gusnocki, take me to the beer right now or I will make you two inches shorter." ordered Max. The Nocks meekly responded, "Right this way Mr. Boyle." They walked a few steps into the darkness, away from the bonfire, to the keg of ice-cold beer.

Mr. Petterson took the pause in Max the Axe's bellicose verbal abuse and said, "Mark, we wanted to come out tonight and say a proper goodbye to you, we want to wish you well and Godspeed." Mr. Petterson's kind words visibly touched Mark. He replied "Thank you Mr. Petterson, that means a lot to me." Noodles said "That goes for me too Mark, I want to wish you the best. Please stay safe."

Mark looked at his old football coach and said, "I'm so sorry I screwed up and let you down." Noodles replied, "You haven't let me down Mark. Fact is, you inspired everyone with your leadership, your passion, your pursuit of excellence. You breathed life into the team, me, and the entire school district. We'll miss you badly. I'll never forget the way you played in the game against Sparta. I never saw a football game where one player dominated an entire team like you did. And they were an elite football team."

Max re-appeared from the darkness voice first with the exclamation "Move aside you morons" as he cut his way into the circle and astonishing everyone with the sight of his carrying four cups of beer. "Monoly," he announced, "We came here to have a beer with you now that you are an enlisted man in the United States Army. And to the rest of you goofballs," he yelled, "this stays here. We don't want your mommies and daddies finding out we came here tonight. If one word of this gets out, I will hunt down and maim every one of you."

He continued his threats, "Brennan! If anybody, and I mean anybody hears about this, then the hospital better have plenty of body casts ready to go, Gusnocki will be first to need one. I'll break every bone in his body just for fun. I've got a message to the rest of you, who I like even less than I do Gusnocki, don't dare cross me. If you do, you'll wish you were Gusnocki after I get done with you."

Brenna's eyes opened wide with fear and her mouth opened in shock, she'd never heard Max address anybody gruffly before, a tone he reserved for boys. Nocks put his arm around her protectively before she reacted and he said straight up and sincerely, "Mr. Boyle, there aren't any Larry Cadodees in this group. You wouldn't have come out here tonight if you thought different. We think it's great that you and Mr. Petterson and Coach Cadwell came to say goodbye to Mark. We're good here, nobody will ever say anything about you teachers coming out here tonight. You've got our word on it."

"Mark, the other teachers wanted to say goodbye and wish you the best" Noodles said. "But they're afraid of the school board right now." "They know this isn't right. The teachers say you've been an outstanding student and this Horace Clark incident is just crap." Max the Axe chimed in "The rest of these teachers, they're a bunch of chickenshits. As for Horace Clark, there's your Larry Cadodee." That was pure Max the Axe and it elicited a tension relieving laugh from the students. Now at ease, they pressed in to listen to the teachers.

"Monoly you take care of yourself," Max gruffly warned as he sipped the last of his beer. Mark answered in a quiet and shaky voice, "I'm sure I'm going to Vietnam Mr. Boyle." Max replied, "Listen Monoly, they only send the best to combat, so I'm certain they'll send a goofball like to Alaska to guard the penguins in some god-forsaken outpost. Don't forget to pack your warm socks." Mark laughed at the thought and Mr. Boyle smiled. Sadly, Everyone, especially Boyle, knew that wasn't true. Mark was correct, we knew draftees were the first sent to Vietnam."

The three teachers finished up making small talk with Mark over their beers and ended the night with handshakes and hugs. When they got into their car Max the Axe turned back and admonished the gang one more time yelling, "Remember, a body cast for Gusnocki if any of you big blabbermouths mess up Mr. Petterson's teaching career here." That said, they got into their car. We watched as they drove off into the night."

Darby broke the silence as the teachers red brake lights faded into the woods. "Wow, that was

214

something." "Awesome," replied Mark. "Those guys are awesome."

## Chapter 14 *Basketball and Bibles*

"Dad, I can't believe you were out in the woods drinking beer with your teachers!" said a shocked Molly as she drove us over the last gentle hills on M57. There the rolling landscape flattens out to the plains of Central and Central Eastern Michigan. I scoffed up an unbelievable lie and responded in the most innocent sounding voice I could muster, "I was there Molly but you know I was an extra wonderful kid so I brought a couple of bottles of Coca Cola along for myself." Molly rolled her eyes and said, her voice dripping with sarcasm, "Yeah, right." "But I will tell you this Molly, and no kidding about it," I continued, "You're the first person I ever dared tell about the 3 teachers coming to the grasser. It's been 40 years but if Max the Axe were alive today, he would hunt me down and put me in a body cast if he found out I told you he was out in the boonies drinking a beer with a bunch of teenagers."

As our little Jeep headed down the road, we caught our first glimpse of Carson City ahead of us, the steeple of St. Mary's Catholic Church piercing the sky above the trees out on the horizon. "Molly," I say while gesturing to the steeple, "Next to my family, that little Catholic Church was the center of our lives. I felt the presence of that Church every single day in my youth. I attended Mass, not just on Sundays, but every single school-day. Sunday Mass was special and without fail or exception my family, like every Catholic

216

family I knew growing up, gathered for breakfast or brunch right after the service.

There was something extra special about Sundays in the winter. After Sunday Mass and after our late morning family meals, we boys would launch a search to find an adult with the keys to the high school gym for a day of playing basketball. The first teacher we called to open the gym would always be head basketball Coach Miles MacDonald. The Coach loved basketball. He wanted school kids to get as much time playing as possible. The public school gym and St. Mary's Hall were the only indoor sites for basketball in the school district. After the high school closed, St. Mary's Hall rarely opened for sports.

He'd tell us what time he'd be arriving at the gym, and we would create an impromptu phone chain to pass the word on to the guys who played on Sundays. MacDonald would join in and play ball for a while, but many times he'd bring along student tests and papers to grade while the rest of us played. He would always give us a heads up about how long he'd be able to stay and keep the gym open. That gave us time to use the pay phone outside the gym and call around to find another teacher or administrator willing to come down to the gym and take his place. Throughout the day, players played as long as they wanted. Most a played an hour or two. Lots of kids hung around all day. On the best Sundays, the gym stayed open for basketball from early afternoon until late in the evening.

The lighting in the high school gym was soft and reflected gently on the honey-colored hardwood basketball court. The gym walls were cream-painted brick that created a lethargic hue. But the gym came alive every Sunday in the winter with the sound of dozens of basket balls being dribbled and shot by players on the 6 hoops in the gym. The entire place rumbled to life to the pleasant sounds of scores of bouncing basketballs echoing off the wood court and the noise reverberating off the hard walls.

Players entered the gym from the windowless brown steel double doors on the parking lot side. The sharp light of a bright Michigan winter sun amplified by the snowbanks in the parking lot would crack the ambiance of the gym with a white glare. The sudden opening of the doors brought a sharp white light that cut patterns across the caramel-colored floor. It hurt everyone's eyes for a blinding second. But whoever came into the gym and no matter what level of basketball skills they brought, all the players in the gym gave a friendly welcoming shout urging the newcomers to get dressed quickly and come join in the pickup games.

There were never too many basketball players. Being in that select group in the high school gym on a frosty winter day was a bonding experience. Some students would get frustrated with the "call your own foul" rules. In those rare cases, a teacher might step in. It rarely happened, but adults might get into a little dust up. At the very worst, an emotional player would leave the gym and declare they'd never play with so-and-so again. A few weeks later, those involved resolved their differences.   The combatants would make amends and be back playing Sunday basketball. Small-town living heals all but the most serious grudges.

A handful of teachers and a few basketball loving adults from around the school district would join the kids playing basketball.  They were the best players, most of them showed up in the evening.  When they played, the competition was the best.  The littler kids would try to get into those games and do their level best to bring a serious challenge.  The older players let the younger players in as much as possible.  They wanted to teach the youngsters how to play good, fundamental basketball so they'd develop excellent basketball skills for the high school teams in a few years hence.  In the gym on Sundays, matching up with the best competition around, the boys of the class of 1970 got as much experience playing basketball as they could within the limitations of a small rural town.

Ever since the boys of the class of 1970 started playing organized basketball in the 6th grade, the word got around Carson City that our class's destiny was to be a special team.  In the 6th grade we were told when we got to high school, we'd make a run at a state championship.

This was pretty heady stuff because no state championship team in any sport ever came out of Carson City.  A look at the small and mostly empty school trophy case showed the last team that had won even a basic conference championship was back in the 1920s.   The basketball season of 1969-70 came with great anticipation, more so than the football team. Where the football team's success had been a big unexpected surprise, the basketball team brought high expectations. The boys established a pattern of winning going 15-2 as freshmen, 17-0 as sophomores, and 15-5 as juniors.

It was only a few days after Mark left for the Army when the high school basketball season started. He had been the star player in all sports, so his absence hurt the team. The 1970 Carson-Crystal basketball team was tall, fast, and talented. Partially because of Mark's demoralizing absence, but more because of sloppy play or to some accounts, overconfidence, the season started as a disaster. The team lost 4 of their first 6 games. The Eagles were not playing up to the high expectations. There were grumblings heard around town. People said the team's coach wasn't good enough.

Head basketball coach Miles MacDonald, a native of Cadillac Michigan, was a crew cut stocky former math teacher who the school board promoted to high school principal after his 10th year of teaching. An alumnus of Michigan State University, he graduated on a full ride mathematics scholarship. The board and everyone who worked with him liked and respected him, including his students. He spent tons of unpaid time in the gym with this group over the years. Mr. MacDonald did this because he was an agreeable guy, loved the game, and he loved winning more than anything.

The unexpected losing streak started wearing on the community, the school, the team, and especially

Coach MacDonald. Before the season started, he let it known he didn't want to coach another year. But the school board encouraged him to coach for one more year. It was the common belief that no one else in the community could bring more basketball coaching experience, MacDonald would be hard to replace. No one wanted a rookie, inexperienced coach to lead this group of talented boys. The administration thought a new coach might not be best for the team, but after much persuasion, MacDonald committed to coach for one more season.

The coach was uneasy with the high expectations. When the season started, his mood worsened with every defeat. The team looked more like their father's clunky Oldsmobiles rather than the flashy Corvettes they expected to be. The boys hated losing, but making it worse was the team's acute awareness that everybody in town was on MacDonald's case because of the team's lackluster start. They all loved the coach and hated it when their losing made him a target for criticism in the community.

Small towns with high expectations for high school coaches to produce winning teams is hard on coaches and players. In a place like Carson City, the hunger for a winning season is acute. For fans of the Eagles, the perpetual disappointments of the athletic teams occasionally brought out the worst from overzealous individuals who were over involved in the sports scene.

Just like in the football season, after every Friday night game, a parent of a player hosted a post game party in their home. Everyone associated with the team along with many of the high school faculty, neighbors, and friends would get together and eat and drink into the wee hours. The football season's afterglow increased the pressures and expectations for varsity basketball. Their sky-high expectations turned into disappointment when the season started off on the wrong foot. The aftergame parties became sources of discontent with MacDonald's handling of the team, and he'd hear about it, there are few secrets in small towns.

Like the football team, the basketball team became the dominant source of conversation around town. Whenever a player or parent of a player picked up the mail, shopped for groceries, filled up the car for gas, ate at a restaurant, attended church, or stepped outside for a breath of fresh air, there was someone who knew them, their family, and everything about them. Everyone wanted to either know what the problem was with the basketball team or offer their solution to stop the losing. There was no getting away from it. The losing at the start of the season was tough on players and tougher on the Coach. One day at practice, the pressure finally got the best of Mr. MacDonald.

At a disastrous practice after the 4th loss of the young season, the players on the basketball team were trying their level best to raise their level of play, but the exact opposite happened. No one could shoot, dribble, pass, rebound, or do anything right. Everything they did went wrong. The offense wasn't clicking. We dribbled basketballs off our feet; we missed passes and errant balls bounced off the gym walls. The shortest, least talented players hawked up rebounds. The shortest bench warmers made the starting five look terrible. Coach MacDonald did a slow burn as every single player grew more and more inept on every successive offensive play.

MacDonald couldn't stand watching this disaster of a practice anymore. The team's ineptitude finally ignited his well-known explosive temper. He stomped out on the court and screamed, "Gusnocki! Give me that god-damned ball. Coach MacDonald, nor any high school coach in that era, rarely swore, so, when he did it was a clear signal that he was nearing the end of his self-control. A MacDonald hurricane started blowing into port.

Point guard Shane Buckley stepped aside and a furious, red-faced Mr. MacDonald took his place, grabbing the ball from Shane so he could show the team the correct way to run the offense. "I can't believe you goofballs can't get this right even though we've been through it a thousand times!" MacDonald screamed at the team. His voice grew louder and more genuinely angry as he had the team run through the offensive scheme. The angry Coach passed the ball to the wing on his right and his voice grew louder and angrier. "Option one the ball goes to the right wing and Tim Fitzgerald; you move your sorry ass through the low post. If you are not open, the ball comes back to the point and over to the left wing to Gusnocki!" he shouted as he caught the ball from the right wing. MacDonald shot the Nocks the ball on the left wing with a two-handed chest pass that would have killed Nocks right there had he not seen it coming.  "Option three!" MacDonald bellowed, "Is to bring the ball back to the point if Gusnocki isn't open" and he waved at the Nocks to give him the ball back.

MacDonald caught the ball from Nocks about five feet atop the key.  Then he surprised everyone by getting even more mad than anyone ever saw him.  He escalated the volume and the intensity by calling everyone by name as dumb, lazy, stupid idiots, and retards.  To make his point at how stupid everyone was he yelled profanities even he never dared say before.  "If the ball comes back to the point on option 3, then you take the f_ _ _ king shot from the top of the key!" and at that point Coach MacDonald angrily dropped kicked the ball towards the basket.

As the ball was arching upwards towards the top of the gym, everyone in the gym froze in fear.  No one ever had seen a tirade from Coach MacDonald like this one. He'd swore at the team a few times before, but introducing the most offensive, profane word was unfamiliar ground.  Everyone on the team was genuinely afraid where MacDonald's tirade was going.

MacDonald continued screaming at the players as the ball reached the top of its arc, almost touching the steel rafters in the gym before coming down in a gentle, perfect arc towards the basket.  His livid voice was piercing everyone's eardrums, echoing off every corner of the gym.  Every guy on the team was trying his best, despite their standing right in the middle of the basketball court, to be invisible.

In those days, we knew MacDonald could grab hold of a player and beat the tar out of us. Back then, coaches and teachers could smack a bit of sense into some screw up without worrying about some parent or administrator getting involved. MacDonald showed, by giving a solid ass kicking to a couple of unfortunate students in school who thought they could handle him, that he was tougher than any of us kids. The wise guys got a good thrashing and established Mr. MacDonald as a proven tough guy. Nobody on the team was ever dumb enough to seriously mess with him.

In that moment, there were only two sounds in the gym. MacDonald's angry, profane voice, and the echo of MacDonald's angry, profane voice bouncing off the hardwood floor and the cream-painted brick walls. An unexpected third sound came like a gentle rain to our burning ears. This sound fit perfectly between the next blasphemous tirade MacDonald was spitting out and the bouncing echo off the walls of his earlier vulgarities. It was the tender sound of the net swishing as the basketball dropped from its high graceful arc down through the basket, all net as they say, and the ball ended up bouncing happily on the floor as if it was interrupting MacDonald's tirade saying, "Look here, I made it, I made it, great shot, great shot!"

Standing frozen like statues, we players dared not to move a muscle for fear of what MacDonald might do. Without moving our heads, our eyes darted to the basket where the coach just drop-kicked an incredible 35-foot basket.  Everyone's eyes bore right back on the coach while he brought the level of his anger up to another                     surprising                     level. The team could see MacDonald's eyes glance, for just a millisecond, towards the hoop.  The coach tried to ignore the fact he'd just made a billion to one shot. He tried to kept his rant going.  But a tiny twitch of his eyebrow betrayed him.  The tiny twitch told the team that the coach realized he'd just made the most impossible shot ever launched in the history of basketball.  To his credit, MacDonald kept going with his angry outburst, but now everyone knew at this point his tirade was more acting than emotional.

The team stood there on the gym floor, caught between fear and astonishment; no one knew what to do as Mr. MacDonald kept on doing his best to keep up this installment of the Angry Coach. The tension finally broke when MacDonald's thin upper lip quivered just a tiny bit.   His act now exposed, everyone on the team started laughing hysterically. Nocks cranked up the laughter even further by looking at MacDonald with the sincerest look and the most innocent tone of voice he could muster and dryly asked, "Coach, I still don't get it, can you demonstrate that play one more time?"

Coach MacDonald wasted his whole emotional demonstration by making that crazy shot of a lifetime. Only God knows how he would have ended his temper explosion without making that shot.   Nocks concluded that "It was a case of Divine Intervention." When MacDonald kicked the ball into the basket, God had stepped in and spared our miserable lives from the wrath of Coach MacDonald.

MacDonald acted as if he could hit that ridiculous miracle shot any time he wanted and mugged an impish smile as the team rocked with belly laughing. He exclaimed with an inflection in his voice that communicated great sincerity. "See how easy this offense is?" He tossed the ball to the Nocks and triumphantly swaggered off the court and into the annals of local lore.


The team straightened out and won ten straight games, winning both the conference and district titles. They won a few games in the state playoffs before being eliminated by the eventual state champions in a regional state playoff game. It was the best team in school history and Coach MacDonald retired at the end of the season, his last year crowned by being named coach of the year.


When the basketball season ended in March 1970, the war in Vietnam took an unexpected uptick. President Nixon had been promising that the South Vietnamese Army was taking the front line in all battles. The Americans starting withdrawing. But Nixon lied. He expanded the war by invading Cambodia. The invasion resulted in an uproar in America. There were protest marches in every major city. College campuses erupted with days of protests so crippling that many schools shut down to let the anger subside.

During this period of great national unrest, the open contempt that Horace Clark held Mr. Petterson in reached a new level. Petterson's teaching methods sparked thought-provoking discussions. The war in Vietnam became a frequent topic in his senior classes. After Mark Monoly shipped out to Vietnam, the emotions and discussions about the war grew more frequent and intense.

Petterson never verbalized his opinions about the war, but he prodded every student about theirs. He kept all discussions objective and dispassionate. Mr. Petterson's disdain for a cliché laden statement would get a student in his crosshairs. But he defended any student who advocated an unpopular opinion from unfair criticisms. Expanding the war affected the students. They became more vocal and active in their opposition to it. That spelled trouble for Petterson.

Over the winter, the monthly school board meetings turned more contentious. Horace Clark and his cronies criticised Petterson without mercy on the choice of books used in the classrooms. It wasn't long before discussions and concerns about Petterson's conduct of his humanities classes came into Clark's rebukes. The conservative members on the board, all members of the Butternut Reformed Church, wanted to know why was it that Petterson's classes were so immersed in discussing the war in Vietnam.

After Judge Lowery coerced Mark Monoly into joining the Army, if there were any students in favor of the war, their voices went silent. The school board meetings grew so contentious that the high school cafetorium became the school board's alternative meeting place to accommodate all the locals who turned out to witness the board and Petterson parry back and forth. Nocks started going to the meetings and organized a growing group of students to join him. The students attended and were solidly supporting Mr. Petterson.

Petterson became the darling of the student body. He symbolized free thinking and dissension. Nocks was one of his most vocal supporters and the main instigator of the frequent vocal eruptions by the students attending school board meetings. Several times Clark answered the groans and boos led by Nocks by admonishing them with the label "Gusnocki's gorillas." Clark's rejoinder resulted in the students booing Clark whenever he spoke. The students began making loud and disrespectful comments about Clark and his supporters during the meetings.

The meetings became dry kindling waiting for the spark that would start the fire. At the first school board meeting after the Cambodian invasion broke in the national news, the students became more raucous and more disrespectful. Clark had been grilling Petterson on the latest book he found offensive. Petterson again defended himself on the selection saying he based his choices on the list of recommended books from the American Association of High School Librarians. But Clark refused to reason.

Clark began. "Mr. Petterson, once again, I say to you, the awful choice of books you are assigning your classes disappoints the school board. These books are not fit for youngsters. Petterson, you are spoiling the innocent minds of our young people." Nocks and his friends reacted. Nocks stood up and encouraged a chorus of boos and catcalls from the rowdy bunch of students sitting near the front of the overflow crowd who came to the meeting.

Clark responded to the outburst and aggressively pointed his finger at the students and saying, "The degrading of our values we're seeing right here is caused by your questionable teaching methods Mr. Petterson, these kids are disrespectful. They are a rabble roused by you. These kids have no respect for their elders. They should support our armed forces and the President, but instead, they are following your lead and have become a bunch of rotten apples."


Mr. Petterson, dressed in his nappy blue 3-piece suit, stood and paused for a minute, then politely addressed Clark and the rest of the board. "Mr. Clark, teenagers have it in their basic makeup to display some bad qualities that you are attributing to being caused by my teaching. I disagree and think I can best refute that by reading you a brief passage if I may," and he picked up a book, opened it up to a page he had marked, and started reading it aloud, "The children now love luxury. They have bad manners, contempt for authority; they show disrespect for elders and love chatter in place of exercise. Would you agree with the writer of that Mr. Clark?" asked Petterson. Clark responded, "That's exactly what you've done to our children. Mr. Petterson, before you came here, our children were courteous and wholesome. You've brought a plague of poor character to our community."

Mr. Petterson responded, "Mr. Clark, I have done no such thing and this quote proves it. The quote is from Socrates, he died in 399 BC. I think it proves that kids are rebellious by nature, it's not Socrates or me that corrupts them. Kids grow through a rebellious stage, they've done that for thousands of years, it's just a natural part of the growing-up process. You and Socrates see the same problems."

Clark's face grew red as he realized he'd been outclassed again by Mr. Petterson's poise and his anticipation of Clark's blaming him for the unrest in the school. "Mr. Petterson, I believe you encourage this dangerous behavior just like you encouraged one of your students to assault me. I am a victim of your teaching methods. I suffer pain and paid extensive medical bills because of your teaching practices. You sir, are a danger to this community."

Petterson smiled and replied calmly. "Mr. Clark, Abraham Lincoln wrote that strong opinions give rise to strong opposition, so unless you disagree with our 16th President, you can see these kids are responding in kind to the extreme positions taken by this school board. I have followed every rule. I have recommended only books approved by respected educational sources, and I've conducted myself as professional as any teacher anywhere."

Mr. Petterson's responses frustrated Reverend Clark and Clark's reddening face showed it. Then Clark made the request that ended up making a fool of the board. "Mr. Petterson, despite the precautions you've taken, it is clear in this board's mind that unsuitable reading material is being assigned to our children. The board will assert its right to reject this material. Furthermore, we want you to bring to our attention any books assigned to these students that is questionable."

Mr. Petterson came to the meeting anticipating the board's wish to become the moral filter for the school. Without missing a beat, he reached into his briefcase and distributed to the board members a two-page report. The document included 30 quotes from the approved literature list that Petterson identified as representative of what "The board may want to review."

Petterson's prepared list pleased Clark. He and the

board members read through it striking off controversial and contemporary authors like Philip Roth. They decided most of the quotes represented books they'd ban from the curriculum and the school's libraries. Petterson abbreviated several of the book titles in the report, including one that the school board banned. "KJVHB" credited to a "collaboration of multiple authors." Reverend Clark and his crew took the bait.

The quote that Mr. Petterson had put to the board was "Yet she multiplied her whoredoms, in calling to remembrance the days of her youth, wherein she had played the harlot in the land of Egypt. For she doted upon their paramours, whose flesh is as the flesh of asses, and whose issue is like the issue of horses." The board wasted little time on this book and banned it as obscene. They fell into Petterson's silent trap. "KJVHB" was the King James Version of the Holy Bible.

A week after the board banned the Bible, an article appeared in the New York Times. Under the headline "Michigan School Board Bans Bible" the Times described the details of the action and included a few board member's names along with Mr. Petterson's. Years later, we learned that Petterson had called an old college classmate who was a reporter with the New York Times. The reporter agreed with Petterson that the article deserved a spot in the national news. We were a community with egg on its face, the only school in America that had banned the Bible for being obscene.

Being labeled in the national news as Bible banners did not set well with Horace Clark and the rest of the school board. Clark hastily called for an emergency board meeting and invited Mr. Petterson there to explain himself. The high school cafetorium was again overflowing with "Nocks's Gorillas" and adults from the community. The vast majority of the audience came to support Mr. Petterson and expected to see the board put on a display of fireworks.

As Mr. Petterson came into the cafetorium, he got a standing ovation led by Nocks and his group of students, clearly embarrassing Petterson. He meandered over to their side of the cafetorium, stood in front of them, then held his hand up to quiet them. "I appreciate your support," he began in a firm voice aimed at everyone in the room. "It's good that you are here, it's good that you are here to see how we govern public schools. The public, including students, has a right to take part in governance. But please, I beg you, please be respectful to everyone here. We must allow for a proper discussion of the issues, even from those with whom we disagree. It is especially important that you allow people with the opinions you disagree with be able to speak to their convictions without fear of intimidation. The opinion you most disagree with might carry the day. Remember that it is better to lose your arguments to the opposition than it is to see a meeting digress to where bullies or fear mongers rule the day. Let's learn from the Romans. Let's not regress to mob rule." That said, Mr.

Petterson walked to the front of the cafetorium and took a chair in front of the stage where the school board members gathered to start their inquiry.

The meeting began with Reverend Clark asking Mr. Petterson "Can you explain to the board how the Bible got put onto the list of banned books?" Petterson stood and replied "This shows the problem we have judging a small segment from a piece of literature and then, based on that small piece, declaring the whole of the work as either proper or improper. The board is now positioning itself to choose between two policies. You're saying, if you decide any part of a book is "obscene," then the entire book is obscene and you'll ban it. The second choice is to hold the entirety of a book to the standard of being fit. To undo your banning the Bible, school board policy has to change to a standard of judging literary works in their entirety, and not on the single passage I gave you from Ezekiel 23: 19-21."

With that Clark lost his temper. "Petterson, I am putting this board into executive session and everyone here must leave now. I expect the board to follow my recommendation that we terminate your contract effective immediately." Stunned, everyone in the cafetorium, students and adults alike started shouting out their displeasure. Clark held his own and exclaimed, "This open board meeting is now closed. The board will reconvene upstairs in the teachers' lounge in 15 minutes for a closed executive session."

Board members quickly left the cafetorium, exiting out a side door to the teachers' lounge. The public meeting end abruptly.

# Chapter 15 *Reflections*

Molly slows the Jeep as we hit the city limits sign for Carson City, my hometown, our destination. The long flat plains of Michigan start at the outskirts of Carson City and extend 130 miles east to Lake Huron. At the city limits we cross wandering Fish Creek, and from the bridge we can see the old wooden dam and millpond on the north side of M57 and the broad wetlands opposite to the south. Molly announced our arrival with "Here we are Dad, the great metropolis of Carson City. It's hard to believe this peaceful little community has such a messy history. And that Horace Clark guy, what a goof, how did the board get away with firing that teacher?" "Molly," I reply, "That meeting lit the fuse."

The day after the fateful school board meeting began with a warm, beautiful Michigan spring morning. Nocks pulled himself out of bed, got up and did his usual before-school morning routine, showering, shaving, having a quick breakfast before making his short quarter mile hike to school. The sun was bright, the air light and fresh, crocus popping up in dormant flower beds in front of the handful of houses he passed as he quick stepped his way to another day at school.

He hopped up the steps of the school as dust covered yellow school buses unloaded outside, exchanging greetings with the kids with whom he was friends. He could see Darby inside the glass doors at the top of the school steps. It wasn't normally a place she'd be this early in the morning. Her face was straining through the glass. Nocks could see that she was there waiting for him. She waved him her way and as he came through the doors. Darby rushed up to Nocks. He noticed she had tissues in her hand. When she got closer, he saw that her eyes were bloodshot from crying. Her voice, always confident and strong this morning was shaky and unsure. She asked Nocks apprehensively, "Did you hear the news?" He nodded and said "Yes, I was there last night, Horace Clark and the rest of those jerks on the board kicked everybody out of the meeting so they could fire Mr. Petterson."

"No no no," Darby replied, her voice breaking with emotion, "not that," and she started sobbing. "It's Mark, yesterday he was killed in Vietnam."

Nocks' mouth dropped open; Darby's words hit him like a thunderbolt. At first, he couldn't breathe, his chest hurt. He almost fell to his knees as an electric shock from the back of his neck to the back of his heels rocked him off balance. With tears welling in his eyes and his voice breaking, he said in disbelief, "Darby, tell me that's not true." But he knew she was telling the truth before he asked, Darby was as tough as anyone he knew, and she was weeping. Cold as she seemed at times, now she reached out to Nocks with her arms open, reaching for a hug. She wanted Nocks to hold her. Nocks felt the same and they embraced, Darby sobbing, Nocks holding her in his arms. He couldn't muster a word of comfort but gently stroked her hair and back, his eyes wide open, staring into nowhere, the both of them devastated by the news.

Mr. Petterson wasn't sitting at his desk looking over poems in his well-worn book of poetry as usual when Darby and Nocks arrived for 1st hour humanities class. Instead, it was Mr. MacDonald sitting at the desk at the front of the room. They didn't expect to see the basketball coach and high school principal; they didn't really know what to expect. He looked up and could tell by the traumatized look on their faces they'd heard the news about Mark.

"Come on in and have a seat." MacDonald said to Darby and Nocks, his voice in a near whisper. All the students in class were crying softly in small groups. Every student looked upset as they talked quietly among themselves about the tragic news. MacDonald stood up from Mr. Petterson's desk and walked slowly to the door of the classroom and closed it. He came back to the front of the room and stood in front of Mr. Petterson's desk with head down and his arms crossed behind his back.

"I believe you've heard the very sad news today about Mark Monoly, but just to be sure, let me tell you what we know this morning. Late yesterday afternoon, two uniformed Army officers visited Mr. and Mrs. Monoly at their home. They conveyed to the Monoly family that Mark was killed the day before in Vietnam. No other specifics about how he died are available, but we know his body is in route home. Mark's funeral is being planned at St. Mary's Church in a few days. The Monoly family will let the school know the details of the memorial services as soon as funeral plans are complete. I wish there was more I could tell you, but that is the extent of what we know at this time."

MacDonald's voice cracked with emotion as he continued. "Mark was a wonderful friend to each of you and I suppose you know this without my saying it, he's one of my all-time favorite students. I have not the skill or wisdom to craft words to bring you comfort or to make his death bring any meaning. I'm sure you're thinking it's not right that someone so young is dead. I share that feeling with you.

Also, I know you're wondering where Mr. Petterson is this morning, the School Board asked that I read their statement to you. "The school board terminated Mr. Petterson's contract with the Carson City School system, effective immediately. We thank him for his service to the school and wish him well in his future endeavors." Beyond that," Mr. MacDonald added, "The school board requests that school employees not discuss Mr. Petterson's employment situation any further. They remind us that if you have questions or comments, they should be addressed to the school board at their next scheduled meeting.

I'm here this morning first hour, my normal preparation hour, to take Mr. Petterson's place until they find a substitute teacher. I talked to Mr. Petterson last night and he wanted me to convey his best wishes to all his students. He also expressed his deepest sympathy to you on the loss of your friend, Mark Monoly.

He wanted me to communicate to you his belief that one reason the humanities exist is to make sense of the chaotic world we live in. He asked me to read this message," and Mr. MacDonald began reading from a yellow legal pad "Mr. Petterson says I've found something that might bring you comfort, a brief quote from Ralph Waldo Emerson. I share it with you as I believe it applies to Mark. "It is not length of life, but depth of life." The class reacted by sitting in complete silence for what seemed like an eternity.

The sound of the classroom door opening broke the quiet. The door slowly opened on its squeaking hinges, and a sheepishly smiling Brenna stuck her head in the classroom. It was the first time in anyone's memory that Brenna was late to school.

She was trying to come into class unnoticed, and that made it clear to everyone that she was oblivious to the devastating news. Mr. MacDonald walked over to her as she entered the room and quietly spoke to her. Although no one could hear what he said, the look on her face showed that Mr. MacDonald had told her about Mark. As she burst into tears, Nocks and Darby instinctively jumped up from their seats and rushed to her. Brenna didn't see them coming and she started wailing, then she turned and ran out the door.

Mr. MacDonald saw Nocks and Darby coming towards him and he nodded his head and looked towards the closing door, showing to Nocks and Darby that he wanted them to follow Brenna and console her.

Brenna was near hysterics and her hurried gate turned into a run as she headed down the hallway to the back door of the school. She flew out the door and started running up the hill towards St. Mary's Church. Nocks and Darby followed her, not saying a word but keeping step with Brenna, not trying to overtake her. They both knew instinctively where she was going.

Brenna ran up the steps of St. Mary's and into the Church. On reflex, she dipped her fingers into the holy water font at the entrance to the Church before sliding into a pew near the back of the nave.

Brenna was sitting in the pew crying quietly when Nocks and Darby came into the Church. They both tiptoed down the aisle and slid into the pew with her, no one saying a word. Nocks sat next to her and slowly put his arm around her. Brenna leaned into Nocks and put her head on his shoulder and softly said, "I knew when he went to Vietnam, we'd never see him again."

Nocks replied in a soothing voice, "I know how you feel Brenna, I had the same awful thought." Darby whispered, "I knew it too. It's my fault he got into all this trouble."

Brenna looked up at Darby with her big brown eyes and said, "Darby, we've talked about this a lot and you know that's not true. I don't believe that, neither did Mark. He said it so many times himself." "That's right," added Nocks. "We know who's to blame. It's that crazy Horace Clark, that dopey Barney Fife, and that goofball Judge Lowrey."

"I don't know if I will get through this," Brenna said as she started sobbing again. "It's just so unfair. I'd do anything to bring him back to us. He was my dearest friend. He was always looking out for me. He never failed to be there for me whenever I needed to talk to someone."

It surprised Brenna, Darby, and Nocks to see Father O'Brien suddenly appear at the front of the Church. He came out of the side sacristy, came to the middle of the altar and genuflected in his usual reverent way, then came down the middle aisle in double his normal gait. He was wearing his full black cassock and white Roman collar. The look on his face was one of concern for the three mid-morning visitors to his Church; he saw them coming from the school from his rectory office.

Father sat down in the pew in front of the three friends. He stared down at his lap and paused for a thoughtful moment, searching for words of comfort. Father took a deep breath before starting, "I've seen lots of grim days in my time as a Priest. Today might just be the worst. These hours spent in sadness linger. The day drags on endlessly." Father kept his head down but glanced sideways to Brenna, Darby, and Nocks and asked a question to neither in particular, "How are we holding up?" "Not so hot," Nocks replied. "We're hurting Father, we're just in a daze." Brenna and Darby nodded in agreement.

Father lifted his head up and turned towards them. "Richard, I've been a Priest for 30 years, I've seen many tragic days before, but I can tell you, today is so painful that I found myself in a daze too. I saw you and Darby out my office window, following Brenna here to Church. It was obvious you'd heard about Mark.

But when I opened the door of my vestibule, I felt myself being lifted from the pain I was feeling. My despair soothed by God's powerful love I feel here in His house. I'm so glad this old Church is the place you came. It's here we search for answers, to find truth, to find comfort. It's the right place to be in moments like this.

While it's beyond our capabilities to figure out why God let this happen, what we can do is comfort each other and trust that God has Mark now with Him, forever to enjoy his eternal reward."

Brenna was the first to speak, she'd stopped crying and had listened intently to Father's words. She thanked him, then said," I feel so bad Father. Mark was so special; I will miss him so much. I don't know if I'll ever stop hurting."

"You will Brenna, you will recover." Father said. "Time passes and each day gets better, God's love for you will heal this wound."

"I'll miss him so much, Father," she repeated. "Mark was so much fun. Plus, I'll never forget the many times he protected me from something bad happening."

Father was a skilled consoler for grieving persons. He knew that sharing fond memories of the deceased would bring comfort to Mark's friends. He asked Brenna with an encouraging smile. "Tell me Brenna, what is your best memory of Mark? Sharing a few good memories will help ease our pain."

Brenna nodded in agreement and thought for a moment. Then she smiled through the tears in her brown eyes before sharing, "When dad bought me the Camero, I couldn't drive it because I'd never driven a stick shift before. Dad was too busy being a doctor, as usual, to teach me. He said I should ask Mark to give me lessons, as long as we didn't drive out of town until I learned how to shift safely. I called Mark and he came right over and soon I was behind the wheel and Mark was guiding me from the passenger's side.

Mark was trying his best to help me but I it didn't go well, I had the car lurching forward, then I'd hit the brakes and I'd almost throw Mark's head into the dashboard, then it'd lurch forward again and he'd slam into the passenger's seat, I'd hit the brakes and snap him back into the dashboard again. He was screaming and laughing and I was apologizing and laughing. We were driving around the side streets of Carson. I had the car lurching forward and then braking it hard. People were watching us, waving and laughing as we drove by. It was so funny and Mark just kept repeating that "You almost have it," and "you're getting smoother," even as he was slamming into the dashboard and back into his seat. We were laughing so hard and I wasn't getting any better at shifting. Mark finally said, "Hey, pull over at the Dairy Queen and I'll grab us a couple of cokes to drink while we're driving around." The thought of coke flying around in the car was just so funny.

I drove around for at least an hour and I'm still not getting how to shift. I pulled the car over and jerked to a stop on the side of the street in front of the school. I told Mark that I'm stressed and need a break. I got out and walked around the car. Mark sat in the car, looking at me from the passenger's seat. I pulled open his door and told him that "You need to take a turn driving. I'll watch you drive and maybe I can catch on that way." Mark gave me a quick OK and jumped out of the car. He happily skipped around the car and got into the driver's seat. We both buckled up and he started the car.

Now Mark had the car grinding gears, the engine roaring, the tires screeching as it lurched forward, then he'd hit the brakes and throw my head into the dashboard, then the car would lurch forward again and I'd slam into the passengers seat, then he'd hit the brakes again and the force would throw me back into the dashboard again.

At first, I thought he was messing around with me and I asked him, "Mark, have you ever driven a manual shift car?" He answered with a sheepish "No."

I asked him why he said he could teach me to drive the car and he said "You didn't ask me if I could *drive* a stick shift, you asked me if I could *teach* you to drive a stick shift." It was unbelievable, he's smiling that enormous smile of his and both of us are laughing our heads off as he continued driving us up and down the side streets of Carson City, lurching, braking, and grinding the gears of my car. I've never had more fun in my life.

After a few hours driving around town, we were both able to shift the car effortlessly. The next day at school Mark told me being my ride had bruised him badly. He also said his stomach hurt from our non-stop laughing. He gave me a nickname from his so-called driving lesson, "Smooth Brenna." I did the same for him and renamed him Mr. Whip Lash.

What I remember most about that day was the sweet way he described his reasons for accepting my invitation to teach me how to drive a stick shift. He said he couldn't say no to driving around town in the coolest car with the coolest girl in Carson. He had a gift to make everyone feel good. It was his greatest talent."

Father O'Brien lifted his head up and was laughing out loud. "Brenna, that is so Mark, I can so see him doing that. How about you Darby, what do you remember most about Mark?"

Darby, still sniffling, recalled when, "We were in the third grade. There was this one day at recess at St. Mary's Academy, the first pleasant spring day after a long winter. Everyone, the nuns, elementary students, high school students, even Mr. Jacobs the janitor were outside enjoying the fine weather.

Mark and I were playing together and ended up in the front of the school. We noticed we were the only persons there. Everyone else was behind the school playing games or enjoying the playground equipment. Mark said, "Follow me" and he started running up the stairs and through the front door of the school. I followed him and he headed straight up the stairs to the 2$^{nd}$ floor. Neither one of us had ever been up there and he motioned me to follow him. We snuck up the stairs to the high school.

When we reached the top of the stairs, the second-floor windows were open and we could hear everyone outside. There was a lovely breeze blowing, it felt so good. We went exploring the main aisle. We peeked inside each room. For the first time, we saw the high school rooms. One door had an opaque glass window in it. Mark gave me a look and opened the door. We went inside and it was a small office with a desk, chair, telephone, mimeograph machine, and another door.

We made our way through the office and opened the second door. Inside was a larger room, the nuns conference room. It was just big enough for a conference table with several chairs around it, a small refrigerator in one corner, and I remember seeing Time, Look, and Saturday Evening magazines lying on the table. The reading material came as a surprise. We expected religious reading materials, not this temporal stuff. The nuns break room astounded us. We couldn't believe it, the Nuns read magazines!

There was one more door. We slowly opened it and were shocked to see a sink and a *TOILET*! A toilet, we couldn't believe it! We couldn't image what the nuns were doing with a commode. We looked at each other in shock. Mark shouted, "Run!" We ran out of the office, down the stairs, and back out into the playground.

We were still breathing hard and I said to Mark, "I can't believe it. What do nuns do with a toilet?" Mark, equally amazed with what we found, came up with a plan. "Let's ask our parents tonight and see what they know about this. In the meantime, let's just keep this our secret." We agreed and that night both of us had extensive discussions with our parents about the nun's bathroom we discovered.

When we got back to school the next day, we found that our folks had independently verified, much to our initial disbelief and subsequent surprise, that nuns were women. Mark's mother had told him that, "Underneath those Dominican nun's robes, there are women in there." We had no idea. It was a shock second only to the one we had later when they told us how to make a baby.

Later in CCD class many times I'd get into lively debates with one of the Dominican nuns about something or another. If Mark could get my attention, and no one else's, he'd throw a glance at the nun who would be passionately defending her statements. He'd raise his eyebrows in mock surprise and mouth the words so only I could see him. "There's a woman in there." It would always crack me up. But he knew I could go past what is reasonable debate and verbally assault an innocent nun. It was his way of making me moderate my passions. Brenna is right about Mark. He kept everyone's interests ahead of his own.


Hearing that, Father grinned and chuckled. Nocks and Brenna laughed out loud. Father said, "My entire life I've thought a Catholic education was superior. Now I

249

find out we didn't cover the true makeup of the Dominican Sisters. I might have to call the Bishop on this one! Darby, that's a wonderful story. How about you Richard, do you have a favorite recollection of Mark you want to share?"

"Mark has this big tree that grew beside his house," Nocks began, "Ever since I first met him when we were little kids, we'd spend a summer's day or two climbing in it, like we did at almost all of our pals' backyards. Everybody had a favorite tree we'd climb. We'd been in his tree many times in many summers. Then one day when we were about 12 years old Mark says to me, "Nocks, you've got to come over and climb my tree. I've found something fantastic about it." When Mark described something as fantastic, I'd believe him. He never failed to deliver. So off we went. Mark pulled himself up the tree first.

Mark climbed way past the highest spot we ever before dared to go. I stayed on a solid branch high up and watched. Mark climbed further up where the branches got smaller and thinner until he reached the top of the tree. Those last few feet he was grabbing multiple thin branches and was pulling them together so they would hold his weight. He yelled down at me and said, "I can pop my head out of the top of the tree. You can see for miles up here."

I couldn't believe what he was doing, we'd never been that high in any tree before and we hadn't used the thinnest tree limbs pulled together to climb up like that either.

After a few minutes Mark climbed down to my branch and said "Your turn" and gestured me towards the top. I couldn't believe that I could climb that high. I was so scared, but Mark was below the whole time encouraging me.

A tree climbing revelation hit me when I stuck my head out of the top of that tree. I never gave much thought about tree climbing. But when you think about it, every time you climb a tree, you are in the tree's shade. You can never ascend a tree in bright sunshine.

My head popped out of the top of the tree and the sun hit my face and the summer breeze blew in my hair. The view from the top of the tree was unbelievable. I could see over the rooftops of every house in Carson City, out past the city limits to the farms and woods. I could see all the way to the horizon. From the top of the tree I could see the O'Conner farm house and their barn a full five miles to the southeast, same for the Magee farm eight miles to the southwest, both in clear sight. I didn't dare turn around and look north, the branches I stood on were very thin, I didn't want to chance                    a                    fall.
The view from the top of the tree was an unbelievable experience. I was literally sticking my head out the top of the tree at its highest point. My view went from obstructed to having not one thing blocking my vision. It was exhilarating, like flying or meeting God or something.

Mark was such an adventurer, he was fearless. His courage and curiosity would rub off on me and everyone around him, just like it did when we climbed that tree. He took me way past what I'd ever do on my own. That's what I'll always remember about him, Father. Mark's courage led me to the very top of a lot of trees."

"That's a beautiful memory of Mark," said Father, "Absolutely beautiful. He was what we used to call a rambunctious kid."

"What about you Father," Brenna asked. "What is your favorite memory of Mark?"

Father O'Brien looked down into his lap once more, his wrinkled brow displaying his deep thoughts. Then he looked back up and said solemnly, "I'll tell you Brenna, one of my sad duties as a priest is coming up in a few days. I have to deliver a eulogy for Mark. It will be very hard to do. I've got so many fond memories of Mark and I'm trying to pick out just the right ones to share for his memorial. I'm afraid this challenge is beyond my capabilities. I'm praying God will lead me to the right words that will bring comfort to our Parish, to you, to Mark's young friends, and above all, to Mark's family. Composing this eulogy, to be frank, is giving me trouble. I haven't decided what to say. If you give me time to sort through them, I'll find the right memory, I'll be including it in my eulogy.

I spent the evening with the Monoly family last night planning the funeral service. The American Legion Post sent a small delegation to the house. They asked the family permission to have an honor guard for Mark. The Monolys agreed. I was so touched the Legionnaires wanting to support the Monoly's regardless of Mark's actions at Boys State that became so controversial. The family and the Vets agreed they wanted the same thing. They decided it would be best to show unity with a display of patriotism. They wanted to take this sadness and use it to reunite the community.

One thing I have settled on is this Richard, I'm asking you to serve the Mass with me for Mark's funeral. He loved you as a brother and I know you felt the same about him. Do you think you can do it?"

Nocks nodded his head affirmatively and replied "Thank you for asking me Father, it will be hard to get through it, but I wouldn't want anybody to serve Mark's funeral Mass but me." He added, "Father, I know you'll help me get through it." Father O'Brien responded, "Thank you Richard. It will be a tough day. I'm grateful that you'll be there to help me get through it too. I'll ask you, Darby, and Brenna that while you're here in Church today to pray for Mark and his family, I ask that you include me in those prayers too. Lord knows I will need His help on this one."

Brenna, Darby, and Nocks could hear Father's voice crack with emotion as he continued. "Richard, I know Mark would want you above everyone else to serve his funeral Mass. The family scheduled the funeral for Wednesday at 10am. I'll see you there."

Father O'Brien stood up and blessed the three friends, making the sign of the cross over them. You kids take all the time you need here," he said, "Go back to school when you're ready." and with that he made his way back up the center aisle of the Church, stopping at the main altar to genuflect, and then he exited out the side sacristy.

# Chapter 16 *The Homily*

Molly slows the jeep down to the 35-mph speed limit as we drive past the two-block long business section of old storefronts in downtown Carson City and come to the blinker light, the only traffic light in town. The light blinks yellow on M-57 and red on North and South Division Street. As she makes the turn at the light onto North Division she comments "I can't imagine how difficult that must have been for kids in high school, to have a friend die in a war."

"The truth is Molly; it hurts to this day. Mark's death devastated us. Not just us kids, but the entire community. But what happened next in our sleepy little town is hard to believe, even after these many years.

The days before Mark's funeral were an emotional blur. At the high school, teachers who tried to continue conducting their classes with routine study plans found their students becoming bellicose when confronted with school work. Those teachers who went the other way and tried to conduct consoling sessions about Mark's death and the war ran into a different wall. They lost control of their classes when students acted out on their supercharged emotions. Before the students could get past their sorrow, they would vent their anger at the teachers with outright hostility. Teachers did their best to calm the kids down, but classrooms were full of students crying and yelling. In every classroom, groups of students would get mad and go home. The atmosphere in school was tense. Teachers, staff, parents, and the students felt something building up to explode. No one knew what or when.

Small towns are usually the best places to live when tragedy strikes, and a small-town parish like St. Mary's is the best of the best. Every time the Monoly family would come back from the funeral home or the Church, women from the parish and the community would have dropped off full meals, ready to eat, often taking time to go into the Monoly home to set the table. They set flags at half-mast at the school, the post office, and the Legion Post. But beyond the many tender kindnesses extended to the Monoly Family by the community, it just wasn't feeling right. Mark's passing wasn't the same as any other community member's death.

Merchants saw sharp declines in business. Few people went downtown for anything other than essentials. Spring sports activities, including practices at the school were all cancelled. There was a sullenness in the air and palpable anger building by the hour at the school. Everyone could feel it.

It took a few days to get Mark's body shipped home for his funeral. His body arrived late on a Sunday evening; his casket accompanied by a 4-man US Army uniformed honor guard. They stood guard at the Burns Funeral home until the morning of the funeral on Wednesday, when the American Legion Post took over the guard duties.

On Wednesday morning Nocks arrived in the altar boys sacristy and went about the business of setting up the altar for the funeral Mass. He lit the candles, made sure the water and wine were out. He put new incense into the thurible, lit the charcoal. When all was ready, he walked across the main altar into Father's sacristy.

Normally, Father would be early, but today he was a few minutes late. Nocks looked out the back door and glimpsed Father O'Brien coming across the lawn from the rectory. He noticed Father meandered off the sidewalk a half step onto the grass, then got back on the sidewalk. When he came through the door, Nocks could smell Father's breath. He'd been drinking wine; something Nocks and the other altar boys saw and whispered among themselves many times.

The Monoly Family was in the front pews of the church when Father O'Brien and Nocks came out of the side sacristy, Father wearing the black chasuble and gold trimmed vestments reserved for funerals. Once the staple of the daily low Mass, the Church had reserved these vestments for funerals and brighter, more eye pleasing colors were being used to "celebrate" Mass. The black vestments are a sober reminder the ceremony coming was the most serious of all Catholic rites. Nocks was there by Father's side in his simple black cassock and white surplus.

The church was overflowing, many people stood in the vestibule. The overflow caused a handful of kids to take the extra seats up in the choir balcony. Most of the persons attending were students from the high school. The teachers and school administrators expected the funeral would bring closure to the shock and anger the students were experiencing. The raw emotions the students displayed led the teachers to encourage students to come up the hill to attend Mark's funeral. They hoped the old rituals would settle everyone back to normal.

Father O'Brien and Nocks stood facing the sad sea of faces as pall bearers wheeled Mark's flag-draped casket up the front aisle to the foot of the main altar. The grief in the still church overpowered many in attendance. Bursts of sad sobbing broke out from all quarters of the congregation from the start to finish of the services.

At the midpoint of the services and following the Gospel, Father O'Brien walked to the lectern on the left side of the main altar to start Mark's memorial homily. His voice was soft yet clear, the church still and quiet. "Today is a day that tests our Faith," he began, "When we believe in Jesus, then a day like today is a day of celebration because we know that the soul of Mark Monoly has completed his journey here on earth and is now with God. Because we are frail and human, today is also a day of the deepest of sorrows as we say goodbye to a son, our friend, our fellow countryman.

The Monoly family wants me to convey to you their ever-lasting gratitude for the many kindnesses extended to them during this difficult time. They want you to know that because their Faith is strong, they will overcome this pain. They have asked me if I might compose this memorial to help all Mark's young friends come to peace with Mark's passing.

I'd like to start by telling you a little about Mark. One of the first times I remember seeing young Mark was at a Cub Scout gathering, back when he was just a tyke. He and all the other Cub Scouts were in high spirits. They were running from one end of the hall to the other, boys being boys. As they raced back and forth, the fastest cub scout fell down and the second fastest inadvertently kicked him in the head when he jumped over him. The rest of the group didn't see the hurt boy or ignored him as they ran by him. The exception was this one Cub Scout who stopped, got down on one knee, and offered to help the hurt boy. It was Mark; he helped the hurt boy up, and in a minute, both ran off to rejoin the chase.

From the start, Mark had the makeup of an exceptional altar boy. I thought he might develop into a candidate for the priesthood. A couple of days later I asked the nuns at school to send Mark over to the rectory and along with him, I asked they send along Mark's best friend too. That's how I came to know Mr. Richard Gusnocki, whom I asked serve this Funeral Mass today, Richard and Mark both came to be my best recruits.

I made an assumption at that cub scout jamboree. I saw Mark's compassion for others on display and expected his best friend would emulate those same qualities. Turns out I was right. Even though both boys were younger than the normal age for becoming altar boys, they were just 3rd graders, both of them responded positively to the opportunity to become altar boys, just as I expected. Both Mark and Richard proved to be dependable, devoted, and reverent servers. I could always count on them, they never disappointed.

For the many non-Catholic friends here today, let me tell you that normally for a funeral we have 5 altar boys. But because Richard and Mark served together so many times and were the best of friends, I decided that Mark, Richard, and myself would celebrate Mass together one final time.

We gather in this Church, with this family, with our friends and neighbors. Each of us come with broken hearts. I can tell you this old priest joins you in grief. I have struggled to overcome my pain to prepare a worthy sermon for you today.

Years ago, I was an adolescent boy growing up on the shores of Lake Michigan. There was a day I remember when my dad took me on a short hike into the wooded dunes, then up into the sand dunes, and finally out to the shore.

It was a magnificent spring day; a mighty wind storm was blowing; the sky was deep blue and half full of bright puffy white clouds that moved fast in the wind. The patchwork of the cloud shadows made the bright blue and green churning seas underneath flicker an eye stinging shining silver.

White-capped waves from the gale were roaring as loud as a thousand lions. The rumble from the breakers was steady, relentless, continuous. We stood there at that beach; the wind stinging our faces, and I felt the power, majesty, and infinity of God. It was, my dad said as the wind was all but blowing my skinny little boy body down the beach, the storm of a lifetime."

Father lowered his voice to a near whisper saying, "That storm came to mind. Today we may find ourselves in another storm of a lifetime. We've had this dust up at the school between the school board and teachers over what books are right. That storm grew dangerous and now we've seen a takeover of the school board by a minority interest who now ruins a fine young teacher's life.

The storms darkest clouds surround us today. One of our own families, the Monolys, come to bury their son who, because he resisted this state of affairs ended up in the most egregious miscarriage of justice, his life now taken by the very War he opposed."

Father O'Brien's voice turned tender as he reminisced, "Growing up in this peaceful little borough, Mark was a boy known for fun, of having a love of friends. He was a lad of considerable athletic talent and a boy who was not one to resist a little Irish mischief. Beyond his love of shenanigans, Mark had a strong moral compass, he possessed an inner voice that guided him to choose right over wrong.

Mark would follow that voice on matters large and small. When it came to the Vietnam War, he let his conscience guide him. He told me many times he opposed war because he learned from Jesus here in this little Church that only God can take a life. Mark hated war because he loved people. He loved everyone and that love set him to action. He spoke out. He did not fear the storm.

Mark discovered under the roof of this very church people would disagree with his opinions and his actions. Yet no one who knew Mark held him to malice. How can it be, we ask, that this boy who was such a wonderful soul end up the violent victim of war? That question, I cannot answer."

Father's voice grew to a crescendo. "We are in the storm of a lifetime. We stand at the beach on shifting sands, our faces sting from the power of the wind. It tests us, the roar of white-capped waves, it drowns our voices. It breaks our hearts. The storm challenges our will. We ask ourselves, where do we go from here? What will deliver us from this storm of all storms? I say to you all, God will. Trust Him. Do not fear the storm."

The power of Father's eulogy stunned everyone in the Church. No one who was there would ever forget Father's call to courage when great storms blow in. Father's empowering words stayed with us.

Father O'Brien then went back to the main altar and finished the formal services. At the end he made a brief announcement "The Monoly family would like to thank you for coming to the funeral today. High school students, please return to school. Everyone else, the family invites you to attend the breakfast courtesy of the Ladies Altar Society at the hall as we adjourn. The family will join you there after the graveside services.

Brenna and Darby could see Mrs. Monoly in her black dress and hat motioning to them as they were filing out of the church. "Girls," Mrs. Monoly said, "I'd like you to come with Mr. Monoly and I to the graveside services. I know Mark would have wanted that." Brenna and Darby looked at each other silently, nodding in agreement.

Mrs. Monoly gave them each a long warm embrace and said, "He loved you both like sisters." Brenna replied, "Mrs. Monoly, Mark was my brother, he always was and will always be."

"That goes for me too," added Darby. They all got into the back of the Burns Funeral Home black Cadillac limousine for the quick trip to the north edge of town to Maryknoll Cemetery. No one spoke in the car.

Father O'Brien and Nocks waited at the top of the steps at the entrance of the Church for the pallbearers when they brought out Mark's casket. The pallbearers, all classmates of Marks, took Mark down the steps and slid the casket into the black hearse.

Father and Nocks quick stepped it from the front Church steps to across the side lawn to the rectory garage and into Father's dark blue 1966 Oldsmobile Delta 88. Father drove fast, speeding wildly along the narrow alleys near the railroad tracks on the north side of town, getting to the cemetery while out of sight of the funeral procession. Arriving before the funeral procession, Father and Nocks walked to the Monoly family plot near the back of the cemetery. There, shaded by a small canopy tent, was Mark's gravesite.

Standing at attention outside the canopy in the full bright sun were eight local American Legion members in full uniform. Glenn Hughes bore the American Flag, six more men bearing rifles, and Max Boyle, the officer in charge. They were waiting at parade rest, waiting to snap to attention for the soldier they'd sent just a few months before to Boys State. They weren't sure how to react to Mark's antiwar stance before, now they came to honor him for his full sacrifice. Max Boyle's baritone voice boomed out "Attention" when the hearse pulled up to Mark's grave and the old soldiers and sailors broke to attention. The mourners got out of their vehicles and walked towards Mark's grave, ambling past the headstones sown among the freshly mowed grass.

Darby and Brenna sat with Mark's parents and family on brown metal folding chairs in the small tent's shade while Father O'Brien and Nocks stood at the head of the flag-draped casket. The Legion Club's Honor Guard came in, folded the flag into a neat triangle and gave it to Mark's sobbing mother, Max leaning in and thanking her for the sacrifice the family had made to the country. Other than her sobs and a gentle spring breeze, the cemetery was silent. The legionnaires returned to the formation outside the tent and Max barked the command to the six men with rifles to fire three volleys in honor of the fallen soldier. The shots rang out and cracked the mid-morning quiet; and after the last volley, the only sound remaining was a gentle Michigan breeze.

Father O'Brien did the final blessing on the grave, sprinkling holy water on the now bare casket. He said a few brief remarks that no one remembers. Everyone quietly moved away from the grave and back to their vehicles, unaware of the events that were transpiring back at the high school.

After the funeral service, Father O'Brien and Nocks went back to the Church. They removed their vestments. When Nocks came out the side door of the Altar boy's sacristy, he saw Darby and Brenna getting out of the limousine in front of the church hall. They joined up and without a word headed together down the treeless gentle slope from St. Mary's church to the rear entrance of the high school.

Nocks opened the school's back-door politely for Darby and Brenna. Brenna entered the school ahead of Darby and she let out a huge gasp and exclaimed, "Look at this! What's going on?" The three stood at the entrance. They saw the hallways were in shambles. It looked like a force five hurricane blew through the school.

Looking down the hallways, they saw every grey metal student locker door hanging open and they saw hundreds of books strewed all over the hallway floors. The three started picking their way down the hallway, trying not to trip on the haphazard mess. Darby stepped over a small pile of books and papers and said, "I don't believe it, it looks like a tornado went through here. Where the heck is everyone?" The three friends zig-zagged their way through the scattered mess.

They passed classrooms and the doors were open. Not a single teacher or student was there. They couldn't find anyone in the classrooms or hallways, even though it was the middle of the school-day. There was no one in the school. With his voice echoing off the empty school halls, Nocks said, "Let's go to Mr. MacDonald's office and see what's going on." Brenna and Darby agreed. They slipped up the stairs to the second floor. There they found the same eerie silence. Same as the first floor, they found scattered books and papers everywhere. No students or teachers were anywhere. They made their way through the fire doors, walking carefully over the debris to the outside of the library next to Mr. MacDonald's office."

"There's the teachers" said Brenna as she pointed towards the closed library glass doors. "Look you guys," said Darby, "The books are all gone from the library." Through the glass doors they could see the teachers in the library. The teachers were all standing in a semi-circle surrounded by empty book shelves. At the center of the circle stood Mr. MacDonald, talking to the teachers. MacDonald cocked his head sideways when he noticed the three students looking into the library through the glass door. MacDonald gave them an intimidating look. The teachers turned around and glared silently at Nocks, Brenna, and Darby. Nocks pulled the library door handle and the three walked in.

"What are you doing here?", demanded a scowling Mr. MacDonald in a sharp tone. Darby looked puzzled by the question and stammered, "We were heading to our classes, but everyone's gone. What happened?" "Where have you three been?" demanded MacDonald. Darby answered, "We just got back from the funeral, Nocks was serving Mass. Mrs. Monoly invited Brenna and I to go to the gravesite services. What's going on, what happened here?" she pleaded.

The unmistakable booming voice of Max the Axe rang out from the group of teachers as he stepped out of the circle, still in his army uniform. He stepped towards the three shocked students. "Your foolish pals came down from the funeral like a herd of stampeding jackals yelling "Book Raid." They went on a rampage and destroyed the school, then they all just walked out of school. Look what they did at the flagpole!" as he pointed his finger to a window of the library. Brenna walked past the teachers to the windows of the library overlooking the front of the school and cried out loud. "Oh my God! Dick, Darby, come look at this" as she waved Nocks and Darby over to the window. They peered out the window to see the front of the school.

They set the American flag at half-mast, the sign of mourning, but it was hanging upside down, the international sign of distress. A mammoth, haphazardly stacked pile of books five feet high and a good 15 feet in circumference lay up to and around the flagpole. The students left, they simply walked off campus. The spring breeze had kicked up and a few open books in the gigantic pile were open, pages flipping in the wind.

Small towns have long memories. The leaders of the book raid are long remembered in infamy. The school board labeled the ringleaders as troublemakers who lacked patriotism. Most of the community residents labeled the scores of participants of the book raid as rabble rousers. The handful of book raid leaders they described as small-town hoodlums.


The larger debate continued for years. What caused the book raid and student walkout? Father O'Brien took blame, his critics said it was his wine inspired eulogy for Mark that lit the fuse. Others said firing Mr. Petterson triggered the student riot. Other opinions included the theory that it was a reaction to the expansion of the war into Cambodia. Others said it was just the seniors in school making mischief.

The book raid participants will tell you to this day that they were angry beyond words with the school board. They were angry that a friend had been taken from them so unjustly by the war in Vietnam. Years later, when a book raider participant got asked, "How could you trash the library?" The common response came back, "How could I not?"

In a few days the community quieted down, students and teachers returned to school, and small-town life eventually returned to normal. The school board and administration tried but failed to punish the leaders. The teachers and administrators hurriedly cleaned up the mess at the school, a process that went late into the wee hours. A few weeks later the 105 students of the Class of 1970 graduated and it turns out, was exceptional like everyone said they would be.

The members of the Mark Monoly's class went on in life and became doctors, lawyers, hospital administrators, nurses, small business owners, teachers, school principals, directors of non-profits, successful farmers, carpenters, and assembly line workers. Only a handful of the class stayed and lived their lives in the school district. The rest moved elsewhere, where the memories of the day of Mark Monoly's funeral would not find them.

# Chapter 17 *The Honor Guard*

Molly is no stranger to Carson City. She spent many carefree days here visiting her grandparents as she grew up. She knows the way to the cemetery as we run north on Division Street, passing under the comforting shadows of St. Mary's Church. The church, rectory, and hall are all unchanged, the church steeple still rusty brick-red and piercing the sky. St. Mary's Academy is long gone, the public schools bought the lot where it once stood and made it into a softball field. They sold the convent many years ago, long after the Dominican nuns ceased being assigned to the parish. Now it's a private home. Molly takes us to the north edge of town, driving past the ruins of the old Central Bean and Grain and the long-abandoned railroad tracks. Our journey ends as she turns our little red Jeep into Maryknoll Cemetery on this cool bright Spring day.

Just inside the silver metal arches of Maryknoll Cemetery, she pulls us over to the side of the gravel lane that runs through the graveyard. We've brought flowers for our visit to her paternal grandparent's graves. It's a brief walk across the freshly mowed grass to her Grandmother's headstone and the brass military marker where her Grandfather rests beside her. We stand over them for a few minutes and place half the flowers on each marker.

Molly breaks the silence and asks "Do you miss your Mom and Dad?" and I answer "Yes, very much Molly,

I think of them every single day." We stand a while longer making comments about the flowers and the neatness of the cemetery on this Memorial Day. After a few moments, she says, "Are you ready to show me where they buried Mark Monoly?"

"This way" I say as we start weaving our way through the headstones. "You know Molly when I was a kid, I came here many times for funerals or to visit my grandparent's graves. I remember walking through here and seeing family names on the headstones I recognized, but the truth is I didn't really know many of the people buried here. I'm thinking that's what you see today, a few names you might recognize, but beyond your grandparents, you probably don't know anyone else buried here. Just like me when I was a boy. Now as I look about this old graveyard, I'm seeing things have changed since my childhood days. I read these headstones today and I know so many of the people who've passed, including my Mom and Dad." I point out gravestones as we pass through, "There's Uncle Kyran and Aunt Alice's grave, there's Max the Axe Boyle. Here are my grandparents. There is Doctor and Mrs. Brennan. There's Jim and Helen Flanagan, over there is Noodles Cadwell. I hear they buried my old basketball coach Mr. MacDonald somewhere near this spot too.

It makes me think when my time comes, bury me here with these people I love, I belong to them."

We come around a few tall monuments towards the back of the cemetery and see a small group of people gathered at Mark Monoly's family plot, just a few steps from Father O'Brien's grave.

A pudgy middle-aged man with salt and pepper hair in a black suit and tie sees us approaching and quickly steps over some small headstones to greet us heartily. "Nocks! It's great to see you" I say as he swats away my outstretched hand and gives me a big bear hug" "Dude", he says with a beaming smile "I'm so glad we finally got you to come to our Memorial Day remembrance for Mark."

"I've heard about it for years", I say "But for no good reason, I've never made it back home on Memorial Day. After all these years, my youngest daughter Molly offered to drive me. It gave us the opportunity to visit Mom and Dad's graves, so I thought, why not? Molly, this is Mr. Gusnocki" I said "Nocks, this is my daughter Molly." "It's Uncle Nocks to you Molly" he says as he wraps his arms around her and gives her a gentle kiss on the cheek, "Molly you look just like your Dad", he says with a wink, "Come on, look who's all here." he says as he leads us over to the small group of old friends standing near the Monoly family plot."

Molly looks back at me with a puzzled look on her face and whispers, "He thinks I look like you?" I laugh and whisper back to her, "That's the charm of your uncle Nocks, he's keeping you a little off balance. Keep your guard up," I warn her, "he's probably planning a prank, he's famous for that you know."

Nocks cries out, "Look who's here" and Brenna in a modest yellow spring dress turns around to greet us with a bright smile, her beautiful brown eyes still mesmerizing. "It's so good to see you," she says happily to me, "and oh my, this must be Molly. I've heard so much about you."

A sharp voice cut in saying, "Molly, you dragged a tired old dog with you today," said Darby as she grabbed us both for a hug. Molly, instantly finding her soulmate with Darby's cutting wit, shoots back, "Oh yeah," she replies tilting her head at me, "he napped the whole way over from Muskegon." Darby, wearing a blue Detroit Tiger baseball hat, red blouse and blue jeans, convulsed with delight at the realization that Molly shares her brassy sense of humor. "Oh Molly," she says grasping Molly's hand and pulling her close "We have so much to share about your Dad! I'll tell you all the embarrassing stuff I'm sure he's never told you."

"Do you remember me?" says an elderly, portly bald man in a tan spring jacket and dark dress pants, extending his hand for a handshake. I recognize him instantly, although he has aged considerably since my high school-days. "Mr. Petterson, how good to see you," I say as I grab his hand with both of mine for a warm greeting. After the infamous Book Raid, the school board reinstated Petterson after losing a lengthy legal process to the teacher's union. As a part of the settlement, Reverend Clark and his cronies from the Butternut Reformed Church were forced to resign from the School Board and pledge never to run for that office again. The community recovered from Mark's death and the Book Raid. Petterson went back to teaching. He became one of the most respected men in the community. For us students, he became the transformative force as we grew to a reasoned and rational exploration of our world. He was an exceptional teacher.

As we shake hands, he says, "It's so good to see you too. Richard and I come here every year, but since we live here, it's easy for us. You've come a long way; I'm sure Mark and his family would be flattered that you made the journey." "That's very kind of you to say", I reply, "Molly and I wanted to come here today, it gave us a chance to pay our respects to my folks and for me to visit Mark's grave. Both of us heard about this mystery soldier showing up at Mark's grave every Memorial Day and we were curious to see him for ourselves."

"He's over there, standing guard behind Marks grave," Said Mr. Petterson as he gestures a few feet away from where we stand. There at the head of the grave, standing at parade rest in a Vietnam era US Army camouflage uniform with a chest full of medals, is a Vietnamese man about our age. He's come to Mark's grave every Memorial Day since 1975. He's always in full uniform and stands a silent, solitary guard this one day per year, rain or shine. The old soldier never speaks or breaks his vigilance at Mark's grave from dawn to dusk.

The anonymous soldier alternates every half hour or so from full attention to parade rest. He's never missed a Memorial Day, nor has he ever spoken. At the end of each Memorial Day he salutes Mark's grave and marches sharply out of the cemetery to his car. From there he drives off to God knows where.

"He's a sergeant" Brenna whispers respectfully to Molly and me, "He always covers his name above his breast pocket. We've taken that as a sign that he's not here for any kind of recognition for himself, but that he's here solely to honor Mark. He's a mystery to us. We don't know any details about his connection to Mark's service. But it's clear this guy loved Mark as much or more than we."

As if on cue, the group all moves closer to Mark's grave. Mr. Petterson asks us all to pause for a moment of silence. Then the old retired teacher read a passage from Shakespeare. "After life's fitful fever, he sleeps well; Treason has done his worst: nor steel, nor poison, Malice domestic, foreign levy, nothing can touch him further."

Then Mr. Petterson brings his annual token to place on Mark's grave, a copy of "Henderson the Rain King." He places it on Mark's brass grave marker, pauses a moment, and steps back into the group. "I've brought something this year too", says Darby, "I found my first communion rosary the other day and I want to leave it here with Mark." She reaches into her purse and lifts out the all-white rosary and places it over Mr. Petterson's book.

Brenna lays a spring flower bouquet on Mark's grave and as she steps back, she says to the group, "I love coming here every year to remember our dear friend, and to see you all again. I have fond memories of Mark and for each of you. We were such wonderful

275

friends." She nods her head toward the nameless Sargent and says, "You know, I believe our mysterious honor guard over there listens in when we share our memories of Mark. I think he's listening in. I believe it's how he gets to know more about Mark's life with us."

"What's your best memory of him", asks Mr. Petterson and Brenna replies without pause, "My memories are the best. Above everything else, I remember how he looked out for me. Once in our CCD class he put his arms around me and held me when I couldn't handle the awful news reports happening in the world. My fears got the best of me and Mark stepped in and his hug made me feel secure. After Mark left school, for the first time in my life, I felt vulnerable. Going all the way back to our days at St. Mary's Academy, he was there to protect me when I needed someone. He comforted me when I had troubles. I've never had a better friend."

"Hey Nocks", Darby said in her most taunting voice "Remember that Halloween night when Mark gave MOST of us sanctuary when the cops took you around town as the trainee garbage boy?" Everyone laughs at the memory and Nocks replies "Believe me I haven't forgotten that I still owe some of you Larry Cadodees a good creaming for that!"

"Who could forget that football game he played in against Sparta." said Mr. Petterson, "I've never seen the community so excited. Mark played the most dominating game I've ever seen any athlete play at any level. It was just like he predicted, it was the night he handcuffed lightning and put thunder in jail."

The End

Made in the USA
Middletown, DE
30 March 2023

27980337R00165